Daddy's Maybe

Denise Essex

B. Love Publications

I dedicate this book to everyone who enjoys black love stories written by black authors!

Acknowledgments

I'd like to acknowledge:

My family: Thank you for allowing me to take up space as an author.

BLP: Thank you for your advice, support, and encouragement.

Editors and proofreaders: Thank you for your patience and all the invaluable information you share!

My accountability partners: Thank you for motivating me with your inspiring goals and holding space for mine!

Me: Thank you for *continuing* to do it, despite your fears. I see you, Goddess!

Readers: Thank you for taking time from your life to play in my world!

Readers Group: A special thank you to Ebony Evans and Fb reader group *EyeCU Reading & Chatting*! This story was developed from a freestyle Friday I wrote in the group's page over the summer!

Introduction

Dear Reader,

Thank you for your interest in my current release. If you enjoy what you read, **leave a five-star rating and review** on **Amazon, and a positive review on Goodreads and TikTok**. Also, be sure to recommend it to your friends. **Follow me on Amazon and** sign up for my mailing list so we can keep in touch.

Mailing list

With Love,
Denise Essex

Sweet Heat
DENISE ESSEX

Prologue

Destiny stood at the kitchen sink as she wordlessly loaded the dishwasher. She had another vivid dream about Xavier Grant. She hadn't seen him in over eighteen years—since shortly after high school—but the same wasn't true in the recesses of her mind. Destiny didn't dream about him all the time, but when she did, it was like her body called out to him. Last night, her orgasm tore her from her sleep, and she had to remind herself where she was.

For a moment, she'd been convinced that everything from her fantasy happened.

"Hey, Mama," her oldest son, Jace, called out. He'd interrupted her lustful thoughts and startled the shit out of her. "Did I scare you?"

Before she could respond, her husband, Jason, ambled into the house and placed a kiss on her cheek. He didn't bother to ask how she was, and she was certain he didn't care. The two of them married for all the wrong reasons. Jason didn't have a solid family growing up, and he convinced himself he'd be happy once he did. Three kids and nineteen years of marriage later, and Jason still wasn't satisfied.

He cheated on Destiny when she didn't give him the endless

attention he wanted. She'd accepted it as one of his character flaws. Destiny couldn't fill Jason's God-sized hole. When they were newly married, she tried, but with age, she accepted it was an impossible feat. In the beginning, Jason got it right in every other area that mattered. He was a financial provider, a present father, and an overall good man. Destiny's standards were always low in the fidelity department. On a deeper level, she was convinced she deserved it.

She loved Jason, but she wasn't in love with him. There was only one man she'd been in love with, and for the life of her, she couldn't shake Xavier Grant from her system. She'd prayed about it and had too many therapy sessions to count, but the soul tie remained.

Destiny turned to face her oldest son. "I'm going to miss you."

"You've got the entire summer to see this face before I leave for college," he said. "We got a new neighbor across the street. Weirdest thing. The mother swore I look like her son Xavier. Other than his eyes, I didn't see it."

Destiny dropped the glass she held in her hand, and the shards scattered across their marble floor. She bent to pick it up as she tried to calm her racing heart. *It couldn't be!*

"You OK, Mama?" Jace asked.

"I got it. I don't want you to cut yourself. Watch your step."

Jace bopped out of the room, confident his mother had the mess handled. Destiny's heart thumped in her chest like a snare drum. She quickly finished her task and walked to the front door to see if she could get a glimpse of the neighbors. *Her* Xavier had moved away from their small town over two decades ago, and she'd never heard from him again. She wasn't on social media because she feared she'd see him and never recover. That was how bad she had it for him after all these years.

She gathered the trash as an excuse to walk to the end of the driveway where the can was. Destiny berated herself for adjusting her fitted shirt and fluffing her hair. The name of the neighbor's son and their physical resemblance were probably a coincidence. Maybe her walk to the curb was a terrible idea. She quickly dumped the trash, praying she hadn't made a complete fool of herself.

"Destiny?"

She had turned to walk up the driveway when an eerily familiar voice floated into her ears. Her hands perspired and her center thumped. *Get yourself together! Just casually say hello.* Destiny turned in the direction of the male voice and almost fainted. He stood wearing a sleeveless T-shirt that put his sculpted arms on display. *Good God almighty!* He held a moving box in his hand, and luckily, it was positioned in front of the python beneath his basketball shorts.

"Xavier?"

He walked to the edge of the curb to get a better look at her. Was there a mist in his eyes? She gave him a small wave and pretended not to have soaked panties the moment her name escaped his lips. Xavier abandoned his box and crossed the street. He didn't say a word, just stared down at her like she was the love of his life.

"Why didn't you call?"

She reared her head back and propped her hand on her hip. "I did call you, but you never called me back."

"After we... you know, you said you would call me, so I waited. The whole week before I left for school, I waited, and you never called." The side of his jaw tightened.

"I spoke to your mom, and she said you made the decision to move early to focus on your transition away from here," Destiny insisted.

He broke eye contact with her for the first time and fell into a fit of laughter.

"What's so damn funny?" she asked and pushed him in his chest. The moment her hands connected with his body, she knew she'd messed up. Shivers ran the length of her spine, and she swore her center did the Milly Rock. *Shit!*

Xavier kept her hand against his chest as he spoke. "My mom never liked you. Said you would be a distraction and I needed to get out of this town. I guess she thought I'd never leave if we stayed together."

Destiny's throat burned. She pulled her hand away from him. *That old bitch!* "I see you got married." Her heart sank at the sight of the platinum ring on his finger.

"You and me both." Xavier scratched the back of his neck at the mention of his wife. He glared at the two rings on Destiny's left hand.

"Kids?" She tried to hide the pain in her voice when she asked.

"A son. Xavier Jr." His face lit up with pride. "I missed you, Destiny. I mean, I was pissed at you until now. I see that my blockin' ass mama is responsible for what happened. But I never stopped thinking of you."

Destiny's eyes stung with tears that threatened to fall from her face. The sadness she wore like a security blanket was back.

"What's wrong, girl?" His voice filled with concern at the shift in her demeanor.

"I need to tell you something."

"OK."

"Mom!" Jace ran to the curb to get her attention.

Destiny quickly dabbed her cheeks and looked up at Jace who towered over her. His hazel eyes bounced between hers and the unfamiliar man with eyes that mirrored his.

Chapter One

estiny Davis in the flesh. Xavier stumbled into his new home, stunned that she was across the street. A cold shower would help him regulate his body. Destiny still looked as orgasmic as he remembered. Her hair was in a natural style, which was different, but everything else was exactly as it was when they parted ways.

"Hey, Double D."

Xavier watched as Destiny Davis slammed her locker and scowled in his direction. She had big titties, but he hadn't come up with the nickname because of them.

"Excuse me?"

Xavier inched closer in her direction and glanced behind him to ensure they had a smidgen of privacy in the busy halls of Tinsville High.

"No disrespect." He tore his eyes from her fitted blouse and caught a smirk on her face when he did. "I called you Double D because of the initials from your first and last name."

"Oh, OK." Destiny Davis's eyes were bright as she craned her neck up to regard him.

"Can I walk you to class?"

"Yeah, but isn't your class that way?" She turned in the direction of his Algebra class. Ms. Witherspoon didn't play about tardiness. Xavier would get detention, but Destiny would be worth it.

She wasn't like any of the other girls at Tinsville High School. They'd been in the same school for two years, and she had yet to shoot her shot. He would catch her gaze in his direction while they sat in the stands at the football games, and she seemed impressed that he had played on the varsity basketball team since he'd arrived, but she never said anything to him. Xavier was spoiled when it came to girls. He couldn't remember the last time he had to put in any effort.

While Destiny seemed impressed with his charming hazel eyes, she held out until he approached her. She was so beautiful that he'd finally worked up the nerve to initiate conversation with her.

"It is, but you have a lot of books, and I thought maybe I could help you carry them."

Destiny's full lips tightened, and she shifted her weight into one of her already rounded hips. Those young hips were one of the first things Xavier noticed about her after he'd seen her alluring face.

"What if those slutty girls who buzz around you all the time see us? They could make hell for an underclassmen like me."

Xavier reached for her books and positioned them under his arm. He didn't miss her pull her lip between her teeth when she saw his bicep flex.

"Don't worry about them. I'm not dating them."

They made their way slowly toward her French class as several pairs of curious eyes escorted them.

"You say that like you're trying to date me." Destiny giggled and tucked her jet-black hair behind her ear. He loved it when she wore it down that way. She took her time to get ready for school each day, and it showed. She wore clothes that fit her body, and Xavier had a hell of a time attempting not to stare.

"I do wanna date you."

For almost twenty years, Xavier was pissed at Destiny. He'd

rehearsed exactly what he'd say to her if he ever saw her again. How the hell could she promise to call and see him off for college and not follow through? Xavier confessed to Destiny that he loved her shortly before he was to move. He was convinced his heart would explode when she'd said it back.

And making love to her had been unmatched. She was his first. And although he had many partners after, nothing came close to the level of passion and stimulation he experienced with Destiny. The first few times they made love were awkward. But after a few months, they learned exactly how to please the other.

He had plans to beg her to move in with him and apply to college where he had been accepted. When he didn't hear from her, he was devastated. Some of the guys from Tinsville High gossiped about how they'd gotten lucky because girls wanted to lose their virginity in high school to nice guys, instead of in college where they might have a horrible experience. Xavier feared that Destiny may have been one of those girls.

But his mother meddled in his business and told Destiny he left for school early. Part of him was not surprised that she was capable of this level of messiness, but it bothered him, nonetheless. Constance Grant had a hell of a track record in the romance department. And because she'd been jaded, she made her son a pseudo husband. She smothered him, but never anything too serious... until this.

How would his life have been had he and Destiny stayed together? He'd sensed her sadness when they spoke. Did her husband treat her like she deserved? Did the household responsibilities rest on her mahogany shoulders, or did they work as a team? Her son was a handsome kid but ran away from them like he saw a ghost.

Teenagers!

"Xavier."

He released a ragged breath as he cringed at Simone's interruption. He was in the shower to get away from everyone. He loved his wife. But the move had placed more strain on their already fragile marriage. When he made the decision to return to Tinsville Heights, she was adamantly against it.

Somehow, she'd overheard him discuss the potential salary with his mentor, and she changed her mind. Her excitement over the money fizzled once she saw the small town with the twenty-five thousand population in person. Simone was a dangerously sexy, free-spirited woman, while Xavier was a simple, principled man. Those differences brought them together in the beginning.

Her unpredictable schedule had served as respite to his predictable work and play routines. It was as though they had what the other lacked. Spontaneity was a foreign concept for Xavier—outside of the bedroom—until he met Simone. She was clear that she had no desire to marry because she abhorred the idea of being tied down.

Part of him was more intrigued since he had no intentions to marry anyone except Destiny. But once Simone got pregnant, he was determined to do the right thing and raise his child with both parents. With time, his outlook on marriage changed.

It was no longer a sacred vow for lovers. It quickly became the stability his child deserved. He and Simone would have to put their needs on the back burner. But after coming face to face with Destiny, Xavier questioned the decisions he made.

Simone was miserable as his wife. She loved him too. It was obvious. But now that Xavier Jr. was twelve and more independent, the need to play house dwindled. Xavier's simple mindset irked her as much as her fidgety attitude bugged him.

Simone didn't want to be tied down, and he was of the mind that if she was that unhappy with her bills paid and her home taken care of, she should leave. It would be her call, because his son was worth the discomfort.

"Yeah, babe."

"Why do you have to say it like you want me to fuck off?"

Xavier's hand propped him up as the water cascaded down the top of his head.

"I'm tired is all. How can I help?"

Simone smacked her lips and huffed out of the room. Simone took Xavier's emotional maturity as his attempt at handling her. He'd just gotten her to stop yelling when they argued. Before their son, the intense arguments led to uncensored fucking. As far as Xavier was concerned, they were long past that now that they had a tween in the house. His namesake would not accept this as normal behavior between two adults in love.

Xavier needed a break before he started the Chief Financial Officer position with the Tinsville City Schools. He'd done well for himself in Academica. He graduated early with his Bachelor of Business Administration degree and continued on to earn his master's in finance. Xavier worked hard but gave credit to all the help he had in his young career. His mentor reached out to him and told him he'd pulled strings to get him an interview. Most CFOs were well into their forties, and the transition wouldn't be easy for him or the small town.

He already had a plan to get the schools out of debt. He had alluded to it in his interview and would get the ball rolling once he was settled. Some of his colleagues would inevitably expect Xavier to prove himself since he was the new kid on the block. Unlike most people, he loved Mondays. That was when he had the most energy.

Destiny hated the start of the work week, but this Monday took the cake. Jace avoided her the entire weekend after he saw Xavier. Did he know? Did he have questions about who Xavier was? Should she initiate this conversation with him, or let him come to her? What would her late mother do?

Now she was forced to attend a meeting with all the managers for the *Upundies* regional branches. Destiny accepted a job at *Upundies* right after high school. Her dream of going away for college would never happen, because she discovered she was pregnant with Jace shortly after graduation. Destiny needed a distraction that would give her pocket money until she could get her degree at the local community college.

She hadn't intended to maintain employment with the boutique style lingerie store beyond the summer. But as her bad luck would have it, none of the local businesses had faith that she could make a difference as a young mother who split her time between work and tending to her maternal duties. *Upundies*, however, jumped on the opportunity to promote her once they got wind of her associate degree in business. They filled her mind with all the success stories of remarkable women whose original job was to stock bras but went on to own several franchises.

The issue wasn't the company. Destiny enjoyed the nature of her work and the brand's blend between sensuality and business. The thorns in her side were her lateral colleagues who were dismissive and threatened by her innovation. She'd forgotten that the quarterly meeting was to be held in her location. Luckily, her employees cleaned and prepped the store thoroughly on Sunday evenings so that the Monday transition would be smooth. They performed to her standards, partly because of how disgruntled she could be at the start of each week.

While Destiny was short, bronzed, and thick, the other women looked the part of the *Upundies* campaigns. They were tall and thin with straight hair that they threw around unprofessionally in meetings. Destiny hadn't received any negative feedback from the high-erups about her natural hair, but that didn't stop the catty managers from throwing shade.

"Destiny," Ivory sang.

Ivory couldn't stand Destiny because she had beaten out her store with the highest sales for the past three months. It was a major sense of contention since Destiny's location in Tinsville Heights had a population that was a third of the size of Ivory's.

"How can I help you, Ivory?" Destiny was behind the desk to

hide from the meeting that would gather in the conference room for as long as she could.

"I just wanted to say how beautiful you look today." Ivory's sentiment didn't reach her eyes. In fact, Destiny made a mental note to walk to her car with someone else in case this woman was as crazy as she looked. She'd watched crime documentaries enough to know Ivory had the right amount of envy to be capable of anything.

Determined not to show any fear, Destiny responded, "Girl, please. What do you want?" She rested her hand on her rounded hip. She was not in the mood for Ivory's perky, passive aggressive antics at a time like this.

Distracted was an understatement. *My son.* Jace always greeted her at the beginning of her day, because unlike most teenagers, he was the first one awake in the house each morning.

He hadn't spoken to her since he saw Xavier at the end of their driveway.

"Collins is announcing who is up for district manager today, and I wanted to say you definitely gave me a run for my money."

She was confident things would go in her favor. Ivory's perfectly plucked eyebrow arched in the direction of her forehead as she awaited Destiny's response.

"Congratulations, Ivory. The job isn't right for me anyway." Destiny rounded the counter and flung her bag over her shoulder. It would take a prayer and the strongest coffee possible to make it through this day.

Ivory and her clique of Barbie mean girls snickered as Destiny found her chair. Destiny was an attractive woman, yet there was nothing more soul crushing than to spend her days with women who taunted and envied her for her appearance. The whispers were about her new hairstyle. Last week she had twists, but she took them down over the weekend.

Destiny once had a verbal altercation where she put an employee in their place for asking dumb questions about how her hair magically grew—she'd added hair when she got goddess braids. After the mention of a discrimination lawsuit and a chat with human resources, if necessary, they decided not to question her about it.

Before the meeting could get in full swing, she decided to text Jason. He and Jace didn't speak as freely as the two of them had, but maybe he'd gone to his father about what he saw.

Destiny: Hey, did Jace mention anything to you?

Jason: About what, Destiny? I'm busy, damn!

She rolled her eyes, unsurprised by his tone with her. She checked his location, and sure enough, he was at *her* house. *Why doesn't he just stop sharing his location when he's there?*

Over the last five years, Jason had gotten sloppy with his escapades. He didn't bother covering his tracks like he had early in their marriage. If Destiny had the nerve, she would bring herself to confront him and do something about his cheating.

The meeting started and dragged along. Out of an hour of time, only about twenty was helpful and necessary. Destiny couldn't wait to get out of here. After the meeting wrapped, she would check on her store and take the rest of the day off. Besides, her assistant was competent and could easily handle things on her own.

"And the moment you've all been waiting for," Dustin Collins, the regional manager for *Upundies*, started. "Our new district manager is someone who needs no lofty introduction. This person has worked diligently for our organization. She's gone above and beyond the scope of her job description and has increased sales for our region from her store alone. Let's give Destiny Cooper a big hand."

Destiny's brown cheeks flushed. Everyone stood and clapped while she sat shocked. She had worked her ass off for her company out of necessity.

Jason worked a factory job after he graduated from high school, but once he was laid off, he never recovered. It was a blow to his ego that obliterated his motivation to seek alternative employment. He willingly received unemployment checks, then complained they didn't have enough for bills.

Destiny found it impossible to confront any of Jason's behavior head on, but she'd be damned if her children would go without. Once she found her footing with her *Upundies* position, he criticized her for working too much. During one of those arguments, she mumbled that somebody had to—it led to one of their worst fights.

Destiny stood with her hand over her mouth and tears in her eyes. Ivory shrieked in disbelief. Maybe if there wasn't too much travel required, she could make it work. *Lord knows I could use the money. And pissing Ivory off is just a bonus!* After her weekend, this news was exactly what she needed.

Dustin Collins told Destiny they would work out the details later in the week. He told her to go home and celebrate the good news with her family. *Family, humph.* She was out of the building and in her car before anyone could change their mind.

She had a coffee in one hand, her phone in another, and her mind distracted. So, when she saw a petite woman with her body close to Xavier's, Destiny's car jumped the curb just before the opening to her driveway. *Crap!*

Thank God for garage doors. The safety of the slowly lowered door hid how mortified she was. Destiny was certain she looked like she lost her mind. Maybe she had. Xavier was married. He had a wife and son of his own.

From what she saw from her vehicle, his wife was stunning. And their boys looked alike, just like their father. She shuffled into the house, praying Jason would stay wherever he was for the remainder of the day, or at least until the kids were out of school.

Destiny and Jason had a child in each of the Tinsville local schools. Jace was a senior at the high school, Summer was their fourteen-year-old middle schooler, and Jason Jr. was their ten-year-old in elementary. They had two weeks left in the school year, and she would relish every moment—because at the end of it, everything would change.

Jace would leave for college in a little over three months. She'd never moved away to college and was therefore unable to relate to the rite of passage. Her mind presented her with every frightening possibility of what could happen if he went out on his own.

Before, she trusted if he was in any kind of trouble, he wouldn't hesitate to call her. They were inseparable up until last weekend. Now he wouldn't even look her in the face. Tears filled her eyes. How the hell they would make it through this?

Destiny stubbed her toe as she dragged herself and her oversized work bag through the door. She quickly changed out of her business casual attire and slipped on her oversized sweats. She didn't bother wrapping her hair because she simply didn't have the strength to care.

Destiny had barely drifted off to sleep when Jason barged through the front door.

"What was so important that you needed to hit me up during the workday?"

Workday? Destiny kept her eyes closed and struggled not to smack her lips. It was the middle of *her* workday. She was under a blanket on the worn living room couch with the television off. *If I pretend to be asleep, this fool will take a hint and leave me alone.*

"I know you can hear me. What was so urgent that it couldn't wait!"

Jason's impatience filled the space around her. She didn't have to open her eyes to know he gaped at her like she was an inconvenience. Anytime she entered a room, he found an excuse to leave. They'd gotten deep into a routine that involved avoidance. And right now, she wanted to avoid him.

His voice and everything about the way he treated her was unacceptable. She stood and glared at him. Without a word, Destiny snatched the blanket and dragged it out of the living room. All she wanted was to take back the past forty-eight hours so she could once again have the relationship she built with her son—her son who was on his way out of the nest.

If her fool of a husband couldn't help her with mending their relationship, he could go straight to hell.

Chapter Two

Onboarding with human resources was a necessary start to Xavier's new position. After hours of online and hard copy paperwork, Xavier decided to drive over to Tinsville High. For what, he wasn't sure. Nothing about the school was as he remembered. The location was the same, but the entire building had been demolished and rebuilt.

He leaned against his SUV as he took in the immaculate construction. This was why they were in debt. Tinsville City Schools were in the red to the tune of twelve million dollars. Xavier had a solution that would not only put them in the black, but the unprecedented approach would likely get the school national attention. He came to the high school to remind him why he needed to take his time.

Timing was everything when it came to a small town like his. Slow and steady was the only way these decision makers would be receptive to his ideas. It didn't matter if what he'd stumbled on was in their best interest. Locals were resistant to change, and as much as he hated to admit it, it mattered who was responsible for new ideas. His fresh face wouldn't work in his favor, so he'd spend the next few months proving himself as an asset.

It was a little before two in the afternoon as Xavier stood in deep contemplation. He saw movement out of the corner of his eye. *Destiny Davis.* She was dressed in sweats with her natural hair coiled like she wore it in twists for the past few weeks. His heart increased as he escorted her hips from one side of the sidewalk to the other.

What is she doing pacing the sidewalk of the high school? Maybe it has something to do with the kid who ran off. His feet had a mind of their own. His brown, leather dress slip-ons clacked against the pavement as he marched in her direction. He was well aware of what his mother had done. She'd been the reason they lost touch.

Destiny's lips parted when Xavier stepped into her space and stood in front of her.

"Destiny."

Clutching her chest, she gazed up at him and said, "Zay?"

"No one has called me Zay in a very long time."

Destiny's eyes were downcast. What the hell had her so-called husband done to her? Not only was she sad, but the fire and sass he most remembered about her was gone. This new Destiny was thicker, but she was also... timid.

He lifted her chin. "Did I tell you how much I've missed you?" He wanted to tell her his wife had been a placeholder for the woman he really wanted, the woman he was sure ghosted him after he gave her his virginity and took hers almost twenty years ago.

"You may have mentioned that." She smirked and created distance between them. "What are you doing here?"

"I could ask you the same question."

When Destiny didn't respond, he continued. "I'm the new CFO for Tinsville City Schools. I guess I came out here to remind myself why I took the position."

"Wow."

The admiration Xavier saw in her eyes made his chest and pants tighten. It had been years since he saw anything but discontentment when his wife looked at him. Destiny had been supportive of Xavier and his goals since they met. Besides how fine she was, it was one of her qualities that stole his heart.

"I wanna go to school for finance." Xavier searched Destiny's face for a hint of laughter or confusion but couldn't find either.

"Cool. What does a finance person do?"

"Donald says the after-school program was cut because of the budget. When I asked who decides how the money is divided, he said the finance guys. I'm gonna be a finance guy."

Destiny had her eyes glued to the million stars littered across the vast sky as they lay on a blanket in a field near her house. Her fingers were intertwined with his.

"Can you do finance and basketball?"

Xavier smiled brightly. He loved Destiny Davis so bad it hurt. He was gonna take her out of Tinsville Heights and give her the world plus seven babies.

"Donald says even if you're really good, you should have a back up plan."

For the first time since they had redressed, Destiny looked at him. "Your basketball coach said that?"

"He did. I'm going to play ball and do money."

"Xavier Grant, I have no doubt in my mind you can do anything you put your mind to. I wish you would do me."

Xavier pulled her on top of him. How she could have a sweet face and such a filthy mouth was beyond him.

"Are you okay?"

There was a hint of sass in her voice that brought a smile to his face.

"I am. Just thinking about how we used to lay out in the field by your house. Do you remember that?"

She held his gaze for long moments. "A lot has changed since then, Zay... Xavier."

"May I ask why you're pacing in front of the high school?"

Destiny's eyes shifted downward once again. Xavier couldn't

help himself. He reached out and tipped her chin until she lifted her eyes.

"I'm debating whether I should pull my son out of class. He's avoiding me."

Xavier didn't have a teenager yet, but he used to be a teenage boy. "Probably not the best idea."

Destiny blew out a breath. "If I don't approach him, we may never make peace. I can't let him move away like this."

Xavier considered his words. "Don't pursue him." He had her full attention, so he added, "Fall back, but be available."

Destiny's brows crinkled in confusion. It was as if their proximity melted his resolve. He reached over and smoothed the wrinkles in her forehead because he couldn't help but touch her.

"What?" Her voice quivered when she spoke.

Xavier had never had an affair with a married woman, but Destiny's body language spoke loud and clear. Her husband did not or simply chose not to satisfy her. He could take care of that for her. *The fuck am I thinking?*

"Boys hate when their mothers try to force them to talk. When he's ready, he'll find you. Let it be on his terms, and he'll feel respected. Trust me."

"OK."

Destiny's faint smile reminded him of the way her kid took off shortly after he met him. He didn't look much like Destiny. He must have taken after his father.

* * *

Xavier had no idea Jace was his. He wouldn't know a truck was headed for him until the tire marks were pressed into his face. In high school, Destiny swore she'd been obvious about how badly she wanted to give her virginity to him. She'd all but plastered it across her forehead, but he was none the wiser. Not much had changed for him in that area.

She couldn't worry about Xavier. She had to focus on her son—their son. He was probably right about giving Jace time. Destiny tended to avoid things, and that made her want to work up the nerve to approach him sooner than later. Maybe she should let Jace come to her.

But Xavier had no idea the magnitude of the situation. This wasn't the time to wait for things to fall into place. She was the adult in the situation. While Destiny fidgeted and contemplated how badly she'd screwed up her son, Xavier's hazel-hued eyes were glued to her body like he wanted to be reacquainted. Was it obvious Jason hadn't given her good dick in almost a decade?

She swallowed hard as her eyes raked across his chest. She could appreciate his hard body through his blazer.

"I should go."

"Did you already have lunch?"

"Do you really think that's a good idea?" She rested her weight in one of her hips as they fell into light laughter.

The size of their town and the rapid spread of true and false gossip meant it was a risk to even stand and have a conversation out in the open like they were. To go out for lunch would mean their spouses would get word that Destiny and Xavier were once again an item.

"I guess not." Xavier placed his massive hands into the pocket of his slacks, and Destiny sighed in relief. The sight of them made her mind reel at the thought of how good they'd feel against her sensitive skin.

Destiny turned in the direction of her car.

"Besides, you'll be seeing a lot more of me, neighbor." When she whipped her head back around, he gave her a wide smile and a wave before he headed toward his vehicle.

Holy hell! Xavier is still the most beautiful man I've ever seen!

Destiny ambled to her car and decided even though she wouldn't take Xavier's advice and wait for Jace to come to her, maybe the conversation shouldn't take place at his school. She would get in the pick-up line for Jason Jr.'s school and then Summer's. Jason often picked the kids up from school, but since she had taken most of the day off, he insisted she get them so he could rest.

She rolled her eyes at Jason's need to rest. Her kids' schools were close to each other, so Destiny arrived rather quickly. As she waited in the ridiculously long line, she felt her phone vibrate.

Please don't let it be work. Please don't let it be Jason. Please don't let it be work. Please don't let it be Jason. She took a much-needed deep breath, then peered at her phone as if her hesitation would have any effect on the sender. It did.

304-555-2469: Do you have the same number?

Destiny didn't recognize the number, but her body responded to what she guessed was Xavier's voice. She blasted the AC to cool her heated state. Jason was a pain in the ass and an unfaithful partner, but she was married, and so was Xavier.

Destiny: who is this?

*304-555-2469: is it weird I know this is Double D from three words? *wink emoji*

There went her panties.

Destiny: you shouldn't call me that

Guilt about the inappropriate nature of their engagement caused her to program his initials into her contacts. Her number hadn't changed since high school; his had.

*X.G.: I still have it like that after all this time? *Umbrella and water droplet emoji*

He flirted with her, and the AC did nothing to cool her heated state. The blare of another parent's horn made her fumble her phone. Jason Jr., who she mostly referred to as Junior, stood expectantly with his superhero decorated book bag and matching water bottle.

Destiny: I have to go

*X.G.: no problem. Later, neighbor. *crying laughing emoji*

It was wrong how right it felt to be near Xavier. He'd been gone for a lifetime and yet they seemed to pick up where they left off.

Jason Jr. plopped in the back seat as a welcomed interruption to her irrational thoughts. He was frustrated he still wasn't old enough to ride in the front seat.

"Everybody else gets in the front, and they're not even as tall as me."

Junior hadn't accepted he was short like his mother, while Summer was tall like her father. Jace was tall like his dad too. Destiny blew out a frazzled breath.

"Hello to you too, handsome. And I'm not their mothers. The law says thirteen, bud. I'd rather you be upset and alive."

"I'm hungry."

And just like that, all was well. *If only things were this easy with Jace.*

Destiny and Summer were close, but she was also officially a teenager. She was taught to say hello to her mother and brother when she got in the car, but after a few moments of conversation, her headphones were in, and she was focused on her phone. Junior had the extra snack Destiny packed for him each day, so the car was silent for the fifteen-minute drive home.

"Can I go meet the new kid?" Junior asked as they pulled on their street.

Crap! Xavier's son tossed a ball with him in the front yard. She couldn't see his entire face, but his profile mirrored Jace's. Unlike her husband's round face, the Grant boys had chiseled jaws like Xavier did when he was that age. *I'm going straight to hell. This is about to blow up two homes, and theirs might actually be a happy one.*

"Let's wait until your dad and I have a chance to meet them."

Junior shrugged, and to her surprise, he dropped it.

* * *

Destiny drove by with two kids in the car. *My Destiny has kids with another man.* The shit didn't even sound right. *She wasn't supposed to get married, and she damn sure was meant to carry my child.*

"Dad!"

Xavier Jr.'s warning broke Xavier from his trance. His hands instinctively went up and caught the spiral headed for his face.

"Where'd you go, old man?"

Xavier laughed at his namesake, who begged to be called Zay J. Simone hated the nickname and refused to call him by the name that was too close to the problematic celebrity.

"I'm not even forty, and you're calling me old."

"Yes! If you were born in the nineteen hundreds, you old as crap."

"Aye!"

Xavier grabbed his son playfully by the neck and tried, but failed not to look behind them to see if he might get another glimpse at Destiny. He didn't. But just as he put his hand on the doorknob, he saw something that stopped him in his tracks. Destiny's husband.

"I'll be in, in a sec, Zay J."

"OK, Pop."

Xavier closed his door quietly and walked with a purpose in the familiar man's direction.

"Xavier Grant?" Jason Cooper, better known as 'Coop,' by the Tinsville Heights Jaguars asked with a smug look on his face when he recognized Xavier.

"Coop, what the hell? You married my woman?"

Jason squared his shoulders and crossed his arms. "Your woman? That fine ass, pretty face, too damn good for Tinsville woman living with you is *your* wife. So how I marry yo' woman?"

Xavier reared back and punched Jason so hard he fell into the recycling bin he stood in front of.

"Zay, what are you doing?" Destiny asked. She'd appeared out of nowhere. Her yoga pants and sleeveless tee made his head spin. He'd gotten over her not calling him for all those years, but she married *him.*

"You married my friend?" The pain in his voice was obvious. He and Coop hadn't been best friends, but they were close enough that he should have known she was off limits. That's why Xavier laid his ass out. Coop had his hands over his face to keep the blood at bay.

"You still haven't slept with Destiny?" Coop asked in the Tinsville high locker room.

Jason Cooper was Xavier's boy, but he had no sense when it came to girls. Xavier had sex with Destiny months ago. He wasn't stupid enough to mess up the best thing that ever happened to him by telling these fools.

It had to be love. He couldn't think of anything but her. Basketball was the only time he could focus. Although there were times when the coach pushed them beyond their physical limit, he would imagine Destiny in the stands, cheering him on like she did at the games. He never got tired with visions of her in his mind.

"A gentleman doesn't kiss and tell, Coop."

Coop threw Xavier a side eye. "You ain't gettin' no cheeks. She ain't even that fine for you to be hanging out of her ass the way you do."

Xavier pulled his clean shirt over his freshly showered chest. "You sound like you want her for yourself."

He didn't have the heart to tell Coop, or any of the other boys at Tinsville, that Destiny told him about everyone who tried to get with her. Coop was one of the many she shot down. Xavier wasn't threatened because he wasn't the jealous type. He and Destiny kept it real with each other. Nothing could tear them apart.

"Zay. That was years ago. We're both married."

The way she whispered the word married brought a smile to his face. She didn't mean it, and she acted like she didn't love that fool. Maybe she did at one point, but she certainly didn't mean it today. If Destiny was a Grant, she would say that shit loud and proud—he was sure of it.

"I'm suing if you broke my nose."

"Xavier, what the hell is going on?"

All eyes flew in Simone's direction. Even though there would be hell to pay, he found immense satisfaction in the envy in Destiny's eyes. She tried her best to conceal it, but she'd always been territorial over him. Simone was a beautiful woman, but she didn't hold a candle to Destiny as far as he was concerned.

"Just saying hello to our new neighbors." Xavier's eyes twinkled playfully as they found Destiny, who looked like she wanted to crawl out of her skin.

"I met Jace over the weekend. You're his mother?" Simone asked with accusation in her voice. The kid was cagey as far as Xavier could remember, but there was no reason to take it out on his parents.

"I am," was Destiny's shaky response. She bent to help Jason up, but he waved her off.

"I'm Jace's dad," Jason said as he reached his hand out toward Simone. He was suddenly preoccupied by Simone's figure. She hadn't asked who Coop was, just Destiny.

She rolled her eyes and kissed her teeth before she stormed off. *What the hell is wrong with this woman? Maybe she can tell Coop is a woman stealing clown!*

Xavier mouthed "I'm sorry" to Destiny then followed Simone. There was something beneath the way Simone regarded Destiny. Maybe she'd sized up the entire situation. In all the years they'd been married, Xavier never entertained another woman, but an hour earlier, he'd texted and flirted with Destiny like the shit was okay.

One thing Xavier was sure of was that Coop got what was coming to him. He'd better thank his lucky stars the women were there; otherwise, he would be on a liquid diet for the rest of the summer. *Destiny Cooper? Shit don't even sound right.*

Dinner was filled with Zay J's stories about his new school. He hadn't had an issue with their small town transition the way his mom did. Simone had a far-off look on her face. Every time he spoke, she glared at him.

He wanted to feel guilty, but they had problems long before Destiny reentered his life.

"The football coach and the basketball coach spoke to me today. I thought I'd have to wait until next year to talk about sports since there's only like two weeks left in the school year, but they were super interested."

Xavier chuckled and reached over and pinched his son's cheek. It was something he started when Zay J was a chunky faced baby. He hadn't been able to break the habit, regardless of his son's age and size. Zay J didn't seem to mind.

"Tinsville Heights sports programs are respected throughout the state. I have no doubt you're in good hands. If you keep your grades up and listen to your mom, you have our support."

Simone kissed her teeth.

"I'm gonna go take a shower," Zay J said as he stood and placed his empty plate in the sink. "Good luck," he mouthed behind his mother's head.

Xavier chuckled and was met with Simone's dagger eyes.

"Are we gonna argue about this, or are you gonna pretend you're not pissed?"

Simone grabbed her plate and Xavier's, although he hadn't finished, and slammed them into the sink. Xavier stared toward the back where their son's bathroom was and waited for the sound of the shower. Once he heard it, he stood.

"That was her?"

"Who?"

"Don't act innocent. Your mom told me years ago that she was so relieved when you finally got over Destiny Davis." She said Destiny's name with a baby voice. He fought not to laugh because she was spot on to be jealous.

Up until they'd moved, he was content being miserable with an unfulfilled Simone. But now that Destiny was in spitting distance, it was only so long before he said fuck this sham of a marriage. Simone deserved to be free, and Destiny deserved to be happy... with him. It was naive for him to think it was that simple though.

"You still want her, Xavier. I saw how you looked at her."

"Do you want me, Simone?" Xavier closed the space between them, but she stepped back.

"You're changing the subject."

"Am I? I didn't forget that you never wanted to marry me. I was okay with it at first. But everything changed once you got pregnant with Zay J."

"Argh!" Simone's golden features reddened.

"I put my kid first. You're pissed like prioritizing my son makes me a bad guy or some kind of deadbeat."

She balled her fists and squeezed her eyes shut. "One kid? Singular?"

"The hell? Yes, we have one child."

"Are you serious?"

He waited for her to finish because he had no idea what the fuck she hinted at.

"You really haven't figured it out?" She let out a frustrated breath and dropped her shoulders.

Simone called him out on his tendency to miss context clues on more than one occasion, but Xavier was content with his need for direct communication. In his book, it wasn't a flaw.

"What are you talking about, Simone?"

She glared at him. "How many years ago did you leave town?"

What the hell did leaving town two decades ago have to do with anything? Is she trying to make me feel bad for potentially loving Destiny after all these years? I hated her, until I came face to face with her again. Crazy how shit comes full circle. Xavier fought to suppress a giddy smile as he considered how he'd end up taking Destiny from Coop's sorry ass.

"Jace is around eighteen," Simone pressed. She squinted her eyes like she wanted to slap some sense into him. But so what, Destiny had an eighteen year old. She had two other kids and a husband, but Xavier was undeterred. She obviously wasn't happy with him.

"Xavier! Jace looks just like Xavier Jr."

The hell? Simone stormed out of the room and left him there with his mouth wide open.

Chapter Three

It took almost twenty minutes for Jason's nose to stop bleeding. The kids wouldn't let up with their questions, so he came up with a lie about how the hot weather caused it. Jace came home in the middle of the commotion but went straight to his room. He didn't speak to anyone and slammed his door when he got there.

Had he seen Xavier punch Jason? Did he think it was about him? Jason snatched the towel filled with ice from Destiny's hands and mumbled incoherently as he also left the room. Summer was on her phone, and Junior was engulfed in a television show.

Renee: hey! Sorry to bother you, but I can't stay and close. I need to leave on time.

This was just what she needed, an emergency at home and work.

Destiny: Where is Desiree?

Renee: I've been calling and texting her nonstop.

The girls' shifts staggered so they could relay information to one another. Destiny looked at her watch. Typically, Renee's relief would have arrived at *Upundies* thirty minutes before the end of her shift.

Desiree was a reliable employee. Destiny's team was full of young women she could count on. If Desiree was unresponsive, something drastic happened. She hoped she was safe and there was a reasonable explanation for her unexpected absence. In the meantime, she would have to close the store tonight.

"I have to go and close the store."

Jason grunted in place of words like a human.

"There's dinner in the fridge. Please heat it up in an hour."

"I know how to take care of *my* kids!"

Destiny's throat went dry. How could he fix his lips to speak to her that way? Sooner or later, everything would come to light. She just hoped the children would come out unscathed.

The weight that rested on her chest lift the moment she was in her car and out of her neighborhood. The secrets from the past threatened to suffocate her. There was a formula to her job. *Upundies* customers were predictable. Work was the perfect distraction from her mess of a life.

* * *

Destiny busied herself with the overpriced bra and panty sets hung on the thin black clothes rack. It was essential that customers saw the items neatly hung when they entered the store. Throughout the day, the underwear would be removed by patrons who had no intention to buy, and it was Destiny and her team's job to quickly rearrange them, to portray a perfectly seductive appearance of the *Upundies* product.

The wooden embossed cabinets sparkled under the store's special lighting. They were accentuated by black clothes racks embedded between the cedar walls and central displays.

"Is it true?"

Destiny recognized the voice before she turned in his direction. She rested her hand on her heart for the conversation she'd dreaded for years. Her eyes could barely focus on him with the presence of new tears.

"He's leavin' for college, Destiny!" Xavier emitted a wail that tore through her. "You kept him from me for eighteen years? You had no right."

"Zay."

Destiny rounded the counter to close the distance between them. The vacancy in his eyes matched the ones all the men used with her these days. Disgust and disappointment peered at her through the same hazel eyes as Jace's.

"I wanted to tell you before you left. But after what your mom said, I convinced myself you somehow knew and wanted nothing to do with me."

Destiny saw the angry outline in his chiseled features.

"After what I went through with my own dad. Bullshit, Dee Dee. Bullshit!"

Dee Dee? It was the softer version of Double D, what he called her when he wanted to express his love and adoration for her. She fucked everything up. The men she loved most in this world hated her.

There was no one else to blame but her. They'd never forgive her for this one.

"I wanted to tell him and let him come to you himself..."

Xavier turned his back to her.

"But I just got married, and Jason thought—"

He was back in her face, bent down at her height before she could take her next breath. "Jason what?" His volume was low and lethal, and his hands were on both sides of her as he leaned against the counter, trapping her. Xavier's proximity frightened and turned her on at the same damn time. He was livid, but unlike Jason, whose indifference was deafening, the fact Xavier was this irritated gave Destiny a sliver of hope that he still cared for her, although outrage over her actions was completely justified.

She swallowed. She wanted to say she was only eighteen. She wanted to tell him she was afraid he would reject her, and she'd never recover. She wanted to admit she never thought he'd return to Tinsville. Destiny shied away from tricky situations, but she would have been charged with murder had Xavier rejected Jace—that shit wasn't an option.

She was also a fool to let her desire to please her new husband influence her ability to make the best choice for her son and his father, his real father.

"I love you, but this is some unforgivable shit."

He loves me? After all I've put him through?

"How could you do it? How could you do it to us? What about Jace?"

Xavier hadn't moved. He whisper yelled so close to her face she could feel the heat of his breath.

Destiny thanked the good Lord the store was empty. They were like star-crossed lovers, desperate to be together but pulled apart by one thing or another. First the interference from Xavier's mother, and now his discovery of an almost adult son.

"I'm so sorry, Zay. I should've—"

"Jace figured it out when he saw me, didn't he? That's why he ran away that day in your driveway?"

She nodded.

"Fuck, Destiny." Xavier stood and placed his hands on his head.

"I'm pretty sure he knows. He won't speak to me. I've wanted to tell him, but every time I attempted, his dad..."

Xavier was back in her face with a glare that made her fearful and aroused once again.

"Ja... Jason begged me not to tell him."

"What?"

"This is my fault. Not your mom's and not Jason's. But it's not like I just said to hell with you. For years, he convinced me you didn't want shit to do with me, and I'd never forgive myself if Jace reached out to you and you denied him."

"I have a mind to sue you and Coop."

Destiny gaped at him. "For what?"

"This shit has to be illegal. Did I put my hands on you? Abuse you?"

She was speechless. She hadn't considered any legal consequences to her behavior.

"No, I did not! But you sure as hell took something from me I could never get back! Either I sue the two of you for pain and suffering or I'm kicking Cooper's ass... again."

Tears streamed down Destiny's face. Not for herself, but for Xavier and her son. The reality of what she'd done was undeniably clear. They deserved to know the truth years ago. She should have done whatever it took to find Xavier and tell him until he listened.

It was illogical for her to assume he would have shunned either of them.

"I want to meet him. For real this time, dammit!"

Xavier left the store and aggressively bumped into a display on his way out. Destiny lost the little resolve she had left.

* * *

"Destiny, you're scaring me. What the hell is up?"

Nothing but wails and sniffs came through on Destiny's end as she held the phone connected with her only living blood relative. Her sister, Tiffany Davis, moved out of Tinsville Heights shortly after their parents were killed in a car crash. They remained close despite Tiffany's apathy toward Jason and her disdain for Tinsville.

Tiffany wanted to leave the state since they were in grade school. When teachers would ask what she wanted to be when she grew up, Tiff would say a grownup who lives in a huge city. Her personality was too big for their town. She was the girl who dressed however she wanted, and people loved or hated her—there was no in between.

"What the fuck did Jason do this time? I don't know why you don't just cut his dick off."

"Zay knows."

Tiffany was silent. Time ticked on as they sat with their breaths as the only sound between them. Destiny missed her sister terribly. She hadn't said anything, and yet Destiny's breathing and tears slowed. The comfort she experienced from just holding the phone with her sister was unmatched.

She'd locked the store up shortly after Xavier left. It was hers to do with as she pleased. If someone complained that she closed thirty minutes early, they could kick rocks with thong flip flops on.

"Dee... you OK?"

Destiny shook her head.

"I'm rolling my eyes because I can hear you shake your head."

A small giggle escaped Destiny's lips. How did her sister do that? How could she get her to laugh when her life had literally blown up. Big sisters were a gift from above.

"I'll sit here until you talk to me, OK?"

Destiny couldn't figure out where to start.

"Why don't you just start by telling me where you are and if you're OK?"

How does she do that?

"I'm at *Upundies*. And I'm not fine. He's so mad at me, rightfully so. If you could've seen the look in his eyes. He said Jace is about to leave for college, and I kept him from his son, even though I know how fucked up he was with Willie Earl living in town and not trying to step up as his dad."

"Sis, breathe."

She did. Destiny's heart rate had picked up at the mention of Xavier's dad, Willie Earl. Xavier told her the ugly truth. He was a product of an affair. Because Willie Earl was married, he never made a real effort to build a relationship with his son.

They spoke. It happened in front of her once, but it was an awkward exchange that a present father would never have with his flesh and blood. She'd put Xavier in a position to be awkward with their son. The tears returned.

"I'll be there this weekend."

"What? You haven't been back since—"

"You haven't needed me since then. I booked the ticket while I held the phone. I don't know how all this turns out, Dee Dee, but all I care about is you and my nephew. Maybe you finally leave Jason's triflin' ass and skip off in the distance with your true love. Maybe not."

"He's married with a son."

Tiffany whistled. "OK. No judgment. Damn."

Destiny fell out in laughter. "Really?"

"Really, what? We wreckin' homes now too? Shit!"

"Whatever. He doesn't seem happy. He said he loves me."

"Baby girl, let's have this conversation in person. You're vulnerable. He's married, just found out he has an eighteen-year-old son, and he has a kid from his current marriage. There's a lot of variables here.

"I'm never going to tell you what you should do, sis, but I want you to consider if your feelings for Xavier are worth the fallout in two households. You have Summer and Junior to think about."

Tiffany was right. Xavier was married to a beautiful woman, and they had their own child to consider.

"I'll be there Saturday at six. Tell Jason I'm staying until you're good."

"You are?" Destiny couldn't conceal the excitement in her voice. Her sister dropped everything to come back to a town she swore she'd never visit again. In the past, if Destiny wanted to see Tiffany, she and the family flew to the west coast to see her.

"Yes. Now go home, have a drink, and get some sleep."

Destiny kissed her teeth. "I thought you didn't tell me what to do."

"Hang up, fool."

Destiny gathered her things. She had no idea what awaited her once she hit her street, but her sister's words and pending visit gave her the strength to face it head on.

* * *

I have another son. I have a son with Destiny Davis.

Xavier had driven himself to the outdoor basketball court near his

33

house, to shoot around and clear his mind. It was too late to be out playing ball in the dark. This had to be the world's longest Monday. He'd gone from seeing Destiny at Tinsville High to texting and flirting with her. He found out she married Coop, and later that they shared a son. His head throbbed.

She thought I wouldn't want anything to do with her or my son. He tried to make Jace's face clear in his mind's eye, but all he could make out was a younger version of himself. What was he like as a baby? Did Coop treat him differently than their other kids? Xavier was sure the kid hated him, because it was clear in the driveway, he had no idea who Jace was.

Destiny was both scared and turned on when Xavier confronted her. He could smell her sweetness through her clothing. It only made him angrier. They should have been together all along. She denied him access to his child and what he knew was the best pussy on planet Earth.

He dismissed that thought as soon as it came. He loved Zay J with all his heart, but he wouldn't be here if Xavier hadn't met Simone. And if he would've stayed with Destiny, there was no way they would have met... *Simone.* She put two and two together about Jace.

Couldn't she have been a tad more sensitive in the way she told him? His heart had more questions than his brain could answer. What would Zay J do when he found out? What if he couldn't forgive Xavier or make space in his heart for a brother from someone other than Simone? *Fuck!*

Xavier got in his car and drove the five minutes to his childhood home. It seemed huge when he grew up, especially since the two-story building was only occupied by him and his mom. Tonight, it appeared to have shrunk. He feared he'd have a panic attack if he stepped inside, but he had some shit to get off his chest with Constance Grant.

"Hey, Zav Baby. It's late. I wasn't expecting you." Her loud voice irritated his ears, although she'd been unaware of her volume since as far back as he could remember.

She stood on the porch with her arms outstretched. He'd stopped by to visit her since he'd been back in town, but she'd been preoccupied with her grandson.

"Why'd you tell Destiny I moved away to college early?"

"Is that what that little heffa told you?"

"Mom, tell me the truth." His teeth were clenched to the point that his jaw ached.

His mother took a seat in a rocking chair with her hands folded on her knees. "I had a feeling about her the first time I met her. She was going to bring you down. You had your whole life ahead of you outside of teeny Tinsville." She rolled her eyes upward.

"You had no right," Xavier said from the bottom of the stairs. He couldn't bring himself to go any closer.

"What does any of this matter now? You have a beautiful wife and son with—"

"Two sons, mama! I have two sons. One with Simone, and one who's about to go off to college."

His mother grabbed her chest. "Lies. That girl is still a liar."

"Shut up!"

"Zay Ba—"

"Stop. You listen to me now, mama. There is no excuse for what Destiny did. I'd take legal action if I didn't think it would do more harm to the kid. Destiny should have tracked me down and told me. But I know for a fact if you hadn't interfered, she would have proudly shared the news of her pregnancy with me. I love her," he admitted.

"You mean you loved her."

"I mean love. I was pissed with her, until I moved back and she told me what you pulled. I never stopped loving her. You wanna hear something funny?"

She stared at him, unsure of how to respond. He'd never raised his voice with her before.

"I only married Simone because she got pregnant. She told me from the beginning she didn't want to get married. She doesn't believe in it. Thinks it's stifling. And now she's miserable." Xavier laughed while apparent sarcasm dripped from his words. There was nothing funny about his failing relationship.

"What?"

"Yep. You were so afraid that I'd throw my life away by marrying the woman I loved too young that you pushed me into a loveless marriage."

"I... Simone loves you."

"You're right about that. She loves me. But she isn't in love with me. She sure as hell doesn't respect me."

His mother dropped her head, and he saw a tear slip from her eye into her hands.

"Jace took one look at me and ran off. He looked at me the way I looked at Willie Earl."

"Enough!"

Xavier slapped a fist over his mouth. He'd gone too far. His mother could take a lot, except when it came to his father. One thing they had in common was when they loved, they loved for life.

Constance Grant never moved on after her affair with Willie Earl. And his father never left his wife. It was as though Xavier's presence was a reminder of the mistake he made. None of that made his mom's feelings for Willie Earl change.

His dad may have loved her too, but he remained married. And out of loyalty to his wife, and his ex-wives, he refused a relationship with Xavier or his mother.

That was the part that scared Xavier about his boys. Would they get along? Xavier's stepbrothers and stepsisters didn't accept him. Xavier once got into a fist fight with his brother because Willie Earl III was embarrassed Xavier said hello to him at school. With a town as small as Tinsville, everyone stayed in everyone else's business. The other children understood they were brothers, but it was a shameful reality his siblings abhorred.

"Sorry, Mama."

Xavier turned to leave. There was nothing more for him to say. He'd said his peace; now he had to figure out how to do what was best for everyone involved, even if that meant never discussing it with his mom again. He would deal with her acceptance or rejection of her other grandson later.

"I saw them in the store once."

Xavier stopped, but he couldn't bring himself to turn and face her. If she was about to fix her lips and say she knew about his son and didn't tell him, he didn't know if he'd ever speak to her again.

"It was years ago. I blocked it until right now. They were in the grocery store on the East end of town. I recognized Destiny right away, but I ignored her. She hadn't seen me.

"But then she turned the aisle where I was, and I saw those chunky baby cheeks facing me in the car seat attached to the grocery basket... the same light, hazel eyes as yours. I dropped a carton of eggs when he smiled at me. He reminded me of Willie."

Xavier's chest tightened. *How could she live with herself?*

"Destiny stared right through me. I figured she would have come out and told me if it was yours. Besides, she had so much going on with her parents' deaths. I imagine I was the last thing on her mind."

"What did you say?" Xavier spun on his heels with his heart in his throat. He loved Timothy and Carla Davis— Destiny and Tiffany adored them. Both their parents were dead? Maybe that was why she seemed sad each time he saw her. "What happened?"

"They died in a car accident a little after you moved."

Anger and sadness for his Dee Dee bubbled to the surface, and he did his best to keep it at bay. "She had my baby without me *and* while she was grieving her parents, Ma?"

His mom lifted her hands as if to say it wasn't her responsibility.

"She was eighteen. If she didn't have her parents, would it have killed you to ask her if she needed anything? Really, Mom?"

He left without hesitation that time. It was hard for him to stay pissed with Destiny after his talk with his mom. Dee Dee was deadass wrong, but his heart softened the more he learned about where her head was at the time. Xavier jumped in his car unsure of where to go first.

He could go home, but he wasn't ready to face Simone. If he saw Coop, he'd be arrested, and the last thing he wanted was to kill the only man his son knew as a father. His stomach bubbled in protest to the direction of Coop raising his son and fucking his woman. How the hell was he supposed to deal with this shit?

As if by some unconscious, magnetic pull, he found himself outside of his old man's home.

Chapter Four

Destiny could barely keep her eyes opened after the amount of crying she'd done. She was off work and parked in her garage. Summer and Junior would be in their rooms. Summer wasn't asleep, but she wouldn't resurface until the morning. Junior was asleep. He couldn't stay awake past nine no matter what went on.

When she entered the house, she could hear a hushed conversation between Jason and Jace. Her stomach lurched. There was nowhere to hide at this point. Her secret was out.

Jace stood the moment she entered the living room.

"Wait. We need to talk," she said to her son. He was much taller than her, but his baby face revealed his true tender age.

For the past eighteen years, she was reminded of Xavier because Jace had his eyes. But now that Jace knew the truth, he had matured, and his disappointment in her was identical to Xavier's. It was as if Xavier Grant was in the room with them now.

"I don't have nuthin to say."

"Aye. Don't talk to your mom like that," Jason cut in. Jason hadn't turned his head, nor had he acknowledged Destiny's presence, but he wouldn't stand for Jace's disrespect toward her. *Maybe he should try leading by example. Disrespectful asshole.*

"You don't know what she did."

For the first time, Jason looked up. He saw her eyes. Destiny had been crying. There were plenty of nights she cried herself to sleep because of their failed marriage or because she still loved Xavier—who she was convinced she'd never see again—but she'd never been this upset.

"Let me explain."

"No! You want me to stand here while you explain to me why I look more like the stranger and his son across the street more than my own got damn daddy," Jace roared.

"Aye, that's enough. Sit your ass down." Jason stood, then paced the floor between them.

Jace did as he was told. Destiny wanted to say something but was convinced Jace would only listen if it came from Jason.

"I knew."

"You knew what, Dad?" Jace's golden features reddened as tears streamed his handsome face. It was obvious what Jason meant, but Jace needed to hear him say it.

"When I met your mom, she was already pregnant with you."

Jace stood and tried to slip past Jason, but Jason held his arm. "I know it's hard, but you need to hear this, Jace. I can't let you place full blame on your mother."

"OK, so you knew. That makes you a hero for taking me in. Why didn't she tell me?" Jace glared at Destiny over Jason's shoulder, cutting her to her core.

"I begged her not to."

Destiny saw the color drain her son's face along with his innocence. He was sick to his stomach, and everything in her wanted to grab him and rock him in her lap like she did when he was afraid of thunderstorms. But Jason was right. Jace would have to find a way to soothe himself through this one so that he could hear the full story.

"Ever since you were a toddler, she'd say, 'we need to tell him'. But I said you didn't need to know. Your mom would insist that I would always be your dad, despite who your birth father is. She said you had a right to know, and the longer we waited, the harder it would be on you."

Jace peered over at her with questioning eyes. She nodded to assure him that what Jason said was true—she did want him to know.

"I didn't want you to look at me differently. Then your brother and sister came, and I was afraid you'd feel left out or something." Jason cleared his throat as he told Jace the facts. "I see now my motivation was mostly selfish, but another part of me feared the day you would want to find him. Then where would that leave us? What if he turned you away?"

Jace wiped his face with the back of his hands. "I need a minute," he said, then left them standing there.

Destiny's eyes were out of tears, but her heart continued to bleed. The two men she loved most, Xavier and Jace, were devastated. She wasn't in love with Jason, and it was obvious he had fallen out of love with her years ago, but she still didn't want him to feel as helpless as he did now. It was one of the reasons she looked away from his many indiscretions. Jason couldn't handle feeling this level of vulnerability; nothing made him feel more in control than fucking around on her. And although he was a shitty husband, he'd been an exceptional father to all her kids.

They stood in silence. It was like the one she shared on the phone with Tiffany, only she didn't feel comforted in this space. Their only bond was the kids they shared together and this trauma.

"I'm moving out."

There it was. It was bound to happen sooner or later. She didn't want to be with Jason, but it didn't make it hurt any less. When he first started cheating, she'd gotten a weird satisfaction from the fact that at least he'd come home to her. Now even that would change.

What would all of this do to the kids? They would never forgive her. She'd made a mess of her life. Jason walked toward her and pulled her into his arms.

"I'm sorry, Destiny. I'm so sorry I let you and Jace down."

His admission broke the last part of her that was held together by a thread. Why couldn't he be an ass in this moment so the separation could be easier? Instead, he was the flawed man who fathered her children. He did his best, but in the end, he missed the mark with her. That was all.

* * *

Destiny woke up Tuesday morning—in her work clothes from the night before—rested against Jason's chest on the living room couch. She remembered him walking her there and holding her close to soothe her until she fell asleep. He must have fallen asleep in the process. She held her watch up and saw that it was seven a.m. She was late if she was going to do two drop-offs.

"Let me. It will give me time to warm up the conversation and let you get a little more rest."

Who was this man, and what had he done to her husband? "Things are never going to be the same, are they?"

He shook his head, then planted a kiss on her forehead. "I'll get them started. You try to take it easy. Yesterday was a lot."

"Tiff is coming this weekend."

Jason stood and stretched his body. "I'll pack enough of my things to last me a few weeks before then."

They shared a small laugh at his fear of her sister. "I'll pick the kids up too. After seeing how devastated Jace was, I need to be honest with Summer and Junior about our separation. I refuse to let them blame you. This is on me, Destiny."

Destiny leaned up because this had to be a hallucination.

"I'm not going to pretend like this is the Jason you'll get from here on out. I'm sure I'll be petty once Xavier and the lawyers get involved. But for our kids' sake, I refuse to put this all on you when I knew you still loved him from the beginning."

Destiny was shocked. Huh? Had she been that obvious?

"Yes. I'm a lot of things, but I'm not blind. I guess I thought, with time, you'd get over him and love me because I was in front of you. For a while, we were good."

"Until we weren't."

"Until we weren't," he repeated. "Can I ask you something?"

"Yeah."

"Why'd you stay?"

"You mean while you cheated?"

Jason nodded.

"I love you."

"I love you, too. But still."

"I guess I felt like I deserved it."

"You cheated on my mom?" Jace asked from out of nowhere.

"Shit," Jason said.

"Jace, baby."

He didn't let them explain. He was out of the door before they knew what happened.

"See why I said I want to tell Summer and Junior the truth? Because of that right there."

Knocks at the driver's side window woke Xavier from his sleep. He'd parked in front of Willie Earl's house with every intention of confronting him, no matter the time of night. He must have fallen asleep while he contemplated how to address the old man. Hazel eyes bore into Xavier's soul as he stared out the window at an older version of himself. He turned the car on and let the automatic window down.

"Your car been here all morning?"

"Sir?"

"You been sitting in my driveway since four this morning."

"No, sir. I got here around eleven last night."

Willie Earl opened the door and waited for Xavier to get out.

"Is Geraldine here?" Xavier inquired about his stepmother.

"Who you think told me you was out here?"

Xavier stood, unsure of what to do next. Should he start talking now? Before he committed to a course of action, the man was halfway up his property. The cane he held didn't have any bearing on the speed with which he walked.

His mother and half the town were convinced one of his many lovers found Willie Earl with another woman and hit him in the leg with a bat. Xavier couldn't be sure if that was just small-town gossip, or the alleged scorned lover's injury was the reason he needed a cane to walk.

"Come on, son."

Son?

Xavier had an hour to sort out whatever this was and make it to work on time, but at the pace Willie Earl moved—fast in his gait, but slow in his communication—he could be here all day. Xavier pulled out his phone and drafted an email to the CEO of Tinsville City Schools. He told him he had a hiccup with his movers, but he'd be available via email or his cell phone until he arrived at the office later in the afternoon.

"Did you come to work or talk?"

Xavier lifted his gaze in time to see Willie Earl disappear into the backyard. He couldn't believe he was here. What the fuck would a visit with him prove? That he was better than his father? They were absent fathers cut from the same cloth, and he was convinced Jace would vouch for his assertion.

He'd walked by Willie and Geraldine's property many times when he lived in Tinsville, but never had he set foot on the property. Xavier could hold his own in a fight, but Willie Earl III put him in his place quickly. There was no way he'd tempt fate and show up unannounced, as a child, after the beating his brother put on him for saying hello.

The fertile five acres of land that held the property were breathtaking. Willie sat at a farmhouse styled table in a shaded area at the rear of the grand single-family home and motioned for Xavier to take a seat.

"You know Destiny Davis?"

Willie sat with his hands propped on his hand carved cane in introspection. "Tim and Carla's daughter. She the little pretty one or the big city, pretty one?" Willie asked with a twinkle in his eye. *Like father, like son.*

"The little pretty one."

"Was sorry to hear 'bout her folks."

"Thanks."

Xavier took a deep breath, unbothered by the slow pace of their conversation.

"I met our eighteen-year-old son this weekend."

Willie said nothing, but his gray eyebrows flew upward. The silence between them stretched. If his dad was waiting for him to state what he needed, they'd be there a long ass time. Xavier had no idea what he wanted or why the hell he was there. But he had a feeling if anyone could understand the position he was in, it would be Willie Earl.

"Thought you married somebody name Simone. Y'all got a son, right?"

With a smile, Xavier nodded. He didn't care how Willie Earl found out the details of his life. Maybe his mother told him. But it touched him that he did, nonetheless.

"You worried about the wife knowing about the kid with Davis?"

"Simone is the one who told me. The kid looked me in my face and ran off. He knew right away. But me... I missed it."

"You ain't worried about your wife or the son from your marriage, what's the problem?"

"What do I say to him? How the hell do I justify being absent for his entire life?" Xavier quietly cleared his throat and stared off at nothing. The breeze from the summer morning was a welcomed contrast to the fire that raged inside him. He could be mad with his mom, dad, and Destiny, but it was his responsibility to step up and make things right with Jace.

Willie Earl shifted his gaze toward Xavier. "You tell him, 'Son, I should've been there for you. You deserved to know me, and I apologize that you didn't. But from here on out, I don't care if you need to yell or cuss me out; I'm always available. You ain't gotta go another day without knowing me'."

Xavier was stunned. Simone could accuse him of not reading between the lines in most situations, but not this one. He was convinced Willie Earl had just acknowledged and apologized to him. His chest swelled. And although he was a grown ass man, the little boy inside of him jump for joy.

Willie rubbed the back of his neck and stood abruptly. "You hungry?"

"Yeah. I could eat."

* * *

True to his word, Jason got Summer and Jason Jr. ready for school and dropped them off. He had no idea where they would go from here or what his preparation conversation with the kids would look like, but he hugged Destiny tightly before he left. If their youngest two didn't suspect something before, they certainly did after Jason hugged her. They were young, but they weren't stupid. Jason rarely touched their mother aside from a quick peck.

His hug was final. It was a goodbye intertwined with sadness and relief. Once they were out of the house, she checked in with her assistant manager to ensure there was no need for her to come in for the day. Destiny took the longest day bath she'd ever taken.

Although the elements of her life weren't ironed out, they were at least out in the open. She could breathe for the first time in years. Xavier knew, Jace knew, Jason told the truth. She soaked her body and the stress melted away. Tiffany wouldn't believe all that went down since they spoke.

Against her better judgment, she reached for her phone. There was a seventy-five percent chance she'd drop her phone in the water because she stayed dropping everything, but she wanted to text him while she had the nerve. She updated his initials in her phone to his full name.

Destiny: *Are you okay?*

Xavier Grant: *I'm still a little mad, mostly hurt. I emailed my lawyer.*

Destiny: *What'd they say*

Xavier Grant: *It doesn't matter. I couldn't put Jace through that*

Destiny: *I'm sorry*

Xavier Grant: *I know, baby*

Shit! Why does he have to text me like this? He still has a wife, Destiny. He still has a wife.

Xavier Grant: *I'm sorry about your parents. I had no idea.*

Destiny: *It's ok*

Xavier Grant: *No, it's not*

Destiny: *How'd you know?*

Xavier Grant: *My mom told me*

Destiny: *Oh. Where are you now?*

Xavier Grant: *You'll never guess*

Destiny: *Somewhere with your other family*

Xavier Grant: *Don't do that*

Destiny: *Well, you have a wife, but you're calling me baby. And even though I know you were pissed when you came to my job, you were* looking *at me, Zay. Like you wanted to have me for dinner. I could tell*

Xavier Grant: *I was looking at you. And I plan to eat you. But shit is complicated. You have a whole corny ass husband too, Double D*

Double D, she could tolerate, but Dee Dee and baby were just a bit too intimate for her at this point. It had been way too long since she had any good sex, and the way Xavier walked let her know he still knew exactly what to do. She had to remind herself that he was with Simone. *He's off-limits. Tiff is right. I'm vulnerable, but he's not leaving his wife.*

Destiny: *Last night, after Jason and I talked to Jace he told me he's moving out. He's telling the kids when he picks them up from school, so we don't have a Jace repeat.*

Destiny's phone rang in her hands, and she almost dropped it in the bath water.

"Hello?"

"Why do you sound like that?"

"Like what?" Her voice was breathy as hell, if that was what he meant. Because Xavier Grant's husky baritone tickled her ears and her naked kitty beneath the bath water.

"Like you're in a pool."

Damn!

"I'm not in a pool. What's up?" Destiny tried her best attempt at casualness with Xavier, but her body betrayed her.

"Where are you, Destiny?"

Ugh! Apparently, it didn't matter what name he called her. If he lowered his voice tenderly like that again, she couldn't be held responsible for using her free hand to take care of the thump between her legs. *Simone! Right, he's married. Stay strong!*

"I know where you live."

"No! Don't come over. I'm in the bath."

Xavier didn't respond for several moments. Destiny moved the phone and saw that the call hadn't been disconnected. "Zay?"

"Look, I'm at Willie Earl's, and I really don't want a hard dick."

Destiny was barely able to conceal the moan that escaped her lips.

"I need to talk to you in person, but I couldn't wait as far as the conversation with Jace. What happened?"

"He said some disrespectful things to me when I got home. You know, after you spoke to me at my work?"

Xavier hummed, so she continued.

"Jason basically intervened, and Jace blurted out what he knew or thought he knew. He assumed I hid the truth about you from him and Jason. But Jason admitted he was aware I was pregnant when we met, and that each year, I said Jace should know about his real father, he begged me not to tell. Jason told Jace that I said each year we waited would be harder for him."

"And where did it all land?"

Destiny fidgeted at the sound of Xavier's gruff, concerned voice, and some of the water splashed over the edge of the tub.

"You alright over there? I'm only a few minutes away."

There was a smile in his voice when he spoke like he got a kick out of making her squirm.

"Don't you do that."

"Do what?" he asked innocently.

"You know what. You're doing the panty dropping voice, but you're married with a young son of your own."

"Give me a sec," Xavier said to someone in the background.

"Is that the pretty Davis girl or the wife?" Willie asked.

Xavier laughed in response and stepped away from the noise.

"Zay!"

"Destiny, you gotta stop yelling my name. It turns me on, and I'm trying to be intentional with you. You know, take my time."

"Take your time, what?"

Xavier sighed. "It's been less than twenty-four hours. Every time I think about how much time I missed with Jace, I get pissed at you all over again. But the fact that I haven't damned you to hell and I even want to speak to you lets me know I still want to be in your space. And..." Xavier hesitated, "Simone and I aren't happily married."

Destiny held the phone, trying to remember what her sister said about married men who never leave their wives. Maybe this was the game they all played. Xavier sounded sincere, but did that mean he would actually leave.

"What am I supposed to do with this information?"

"Why'd you tell me Jason moved out?"

"Because I want you, Xavier. I've wanted you since the first time I laid eyes on you freshman year."

Xavier held the phone, and all she could hear was his ragged breath.

"We didn't start dating until right before junior year."

"I know that, but I liked you all along."

"Listen, I'm cleaning up my life the way I suppose you're going to clean up yours. The main priority is the kids. Heavy emphasis on our kid."

Destiny's heart fluttered at the sound of Xavier's reference to Jace as their kid.

"I need to sit down with him when he's in a better space. Then there's our exes."

"Does Simone know she's your ex?"

"After speaking to my dad, I have a lot more clarity about the right thing to do."

"I don't know what that means, but I feel shitty flirting with a married man after all the women who cheated with Jason, knowing he was with me."

"What? Please tell me this man didn't have the balls to cheat on you."

"He did. To make matters worse, before he took the kids to school, Jace overheard him ask me why I stuck around when we both knew I knew what he'd been doing."

"Shit! We fucked this kid up. Sounds like he hates all three of us."

"Probably." Destiny's eyes burned as she considered her son's fragile state. She couldn't bully her way back into his heart. She had to toe the line. She'd given him the facts; now she had to allow him the space to process. She prayed they'd be in a better place by the end of the summer.

"Why did you let him cheat on you?"

Destiny was ashamed to have this conversation with Xavier, so she changed the subject. "We're talking about Simone who has no idea you're speaking to me the way you're speaking to me."

"She knew who you were the moment she saw you. Simone is the one who told me about Jace. I wanted to talk about this face to face with you, but at the risk of being thrown into the cheatin' ass husband category with Jason Cooper's whack ass, I need to make this clear now. Simone never wanted to be married. She doesn't believe in it, and I was cool with that because the only woman I ever wanted to marry was back in Tinsville."

Destiny's eyes closed, and her heart rate tripled.

"But I talked her into marriage when she found out she was pregnant."

Destiny gasped. What had she done? It should have been her.

"As Zay J grew up and needed the picture-perfect parents less and less, we started to fall apart at the seams. This was years before Tinsville. The size of the town was the nail in the coffin. She hates it here."

Destiny snickered. She'd seen beautiful girls like Simone struggle in their town. Tinsville was full of the same people in each other's business. Destiny could only imagine Simone's face when she saw the local mall. There were so few available stores that the locals referred to it as a small—a small mall.

"And for the record, I've never done so much as texted another woman in the twelve years I've been married until yesterday."

Destiny gasped again. She was speechless.

"I want you too, Destiny. I always have, and I always will. But I gotta make some things right first. We both need to cross some T's and dot some I's before I can act on what I want to."

Her line beeped with an incoming call.

"Thank God."

"What happened?"

"It's another call. I don't know how much longer I can listen to your voice and be on my best behavior, in this bath, when you haven't broken things off with Simone. This is Tiffany, who by the way is convinced you're going to string me along and never leave your wife."

"How did she—"

"Bye, Zay!"

"Damn, OK. Bye, baby."

Chapter Five

Xavier had pep in his step when he left Willie Earl's. They had kept things surface except for his father's suggestion on how to approach Jace. He had a bit of closure when Willie Earl took the opportunity to apologize to him through their conversation. Geraldine was there for lunch, but she didn't speak much. It didn't bother Xavier whatsoever.

The news that Jason moved out put him in a better mood than he was before their call. He didn't know how he and Destiny would tie up all their loose ends. There were a billion external factors, including his middle-schooler who'd never experienced anything semi-traumatic his entire life. The biggest adjustment he'd made was the move to Tinsville, and he seemed to love small city living.

Would he love it after his parents split? What about when he learned about Jace? How about Xavier's proximity to Destiny? Because now that she was available, she would be his again somehow.

With his head jumbled around the way it was, he called the CEO and told him things were a bit chaotic at home, but he would be online for their afternoon meeting. The CEO encouraged him not to worry about the meeting and instead take his time to get settled.

Xavier was encouraged to join them at the start of the following week.

With that taken care of, he decided to head home and see if he could broach the conversation with Simone. He wasn't as worried about how she would take his suggestion to separate as he was concerned for his boys. *My boys!* Zay J would be at school for a few more hours, which would give him and Simone ample time to have an uninterrupted adult conversation.

"Babe, whose car is that in the driveway?" Xavier asked as he threw his keys on the countertop.

He saw Simone lift abruptly from the couch, and a man he didn't recognize stood to greet him. Xavier's arms were crossed over his chest while the idiot reached his arm toward him. *The fuck?*

"I didn't expect you." Simone looked nervously between Xavier and the other man.

"That's the first thing you wanna say to me?"

"I thought you would be at work all day."

"Which means you wouldn't have invited buddy over if you thought I might drop in. What's goin' on? And who is this?"

"No disrespect," this clown said.

"Nah, this is super disrespectful. She's wearing a ring. And you're in her husband's house. You don't have a place of your own?"

"She said y'all was having problems," he responded as if what he said justified them being alone in Xavier's home.

"Jeff." Simone huffed.

"Clear out my house. I don't give a shit what was about to happen, just get out."

Jeff grabbed his keys and stood. Xavier didn't budge when they breezed past him.

"Jeff, can you step outside so I can have a word with my ex-wife?"

Simone's neck snapped up.

"Oh, cool, so y'all are divorced. OK. I'mma be outside until you finish, boo," Jeff said. He was wide, but his legs were weak. Xavier had no doubt that he could lay him out if need be.

"What's up?" Xavier asked as he peered down at Simone once her new man was outside.

"It's obvious things between us are over. I know you have a thing with Destiny."

"Did I bring her to our house when I thought you were gone?"

"No, but—"

"I came home in the middle of the day to have an adult conversation with you about how we start the process of separating."

Tears sprang to Simone's eyes and her fists balled. "That bitch," she mumbled.

"I asked you before if you want me. Do you like living here? Where my job is? Do you want to work this out and go to counseling?"

She hung her head.

"Simone, we'll figure it out. I'll be honest, I've changed. I don't want a roommate setup anymore. I don't want a wife who feels like she needs a Jeff for excitement. I love you."

She kissed her teeth.

"I'm serious. You're the mother of my child, and we've been together over twelve years. Of course, I love you. But are you happy? Do *I* make you happy, Simone?"

Tears dropped down her face as she tapped her foot and shook her head. "I've been unhappy for years. But you're always kind and good to me. Only an idiot would divorce a man because she's bored."

"You deserve more, and I do too. Come here." Xavier pulled Simone into a warm embrace, despite her best efforts to push him away. He allowed her to cry until a knock on the door interrupted them.

"You almost done, Simone?" Jeff asked from the other side of the screen door.

She looked up at Xavier, and they fell into an easy laughter.

"I'm sorry about that. He's kind of an idiot."

"You think? But listen. I know you and I are on the same page. We've had ample time with the reality of our situation, although we were too stubborn to verbally address it. I'm still worried about Zay J though. I have no idea how he'll deal with a separation and a step-brother."

Simone's shoulders sank. "This is why I was OK with a marriage of convenience. I don't know shit about how to help him through this. He's gonna blame me?"

"If he's gonna blame anyone, it will be me. I'm the one with the outside kid... whom I have yet to talk to, by the way."

"Oh." Simone stepped back and smoothed her sundress. "I'm glad I get to have you as my ex-husband and not somebody that's like..."

"Like Jeff?" Xavier asked with a smirk.

"Did y'all call me?" Jeff asked as he once again appeared in front of the door.

Xavier opened it and playfully pushed Simone out. "Here, man," he said to Jeff.

"I'm kidding," he mouthed to Simone. "Can we talk about how we're going to do this with Zay in a few hours?"

"Of course."

"I want us to both be here when he gets home from school."

"OK, Xavier. Let's meet back here at two."

"I love you."

"I love you too."

"Y'all don't act like divorced people," Jeff said as he rested his hand on Simone's lower back and guided her to his vehicle.

* * *

When Jason and the kids got home from school, Summer had an attitude, and Junior looked like somebody stole his favorite action hero.

"What happened?" Destiny asked Jason. She pulled him into the kitchen to figure out if he had the conversation without her.

"Jace texted his siblings and said he's moving out for the summer."

"What?"

"My dad called and said he's fine with Jace staying with him until we work everything out."

Destiny's phone vibrated. She hoped it was Jace. If she could just get twenty minutes alone with him, she'd answer any questions he had. She'd explain the situation as best as she could.

Xavier Grant: I came home to talk to Simone and met her new man

What in the name of everything unholy?

Destiny: I'm about to talk to Summer and Junior before Jason leaves for the night.

Xavier Grant: Good luck

Destiny: Thank you

Xavier Grant: Will you call me later?

"Destiny!"

"Yeah, my bad." She hoped the blush on her face wasn't obvious.

"Can you at least let me leave before you make plans?"

"You mean respect you like you did me all this time?"

Jason stared at her wordlessly. She hadn't meant to openly flirt in his face, but her emotions were all over the place. If she could work things out with her kids, to hell with what anyone else thought. Destiny wanted Xavier, and she was giddy as hell about what might go down when they could finally be alone.

"I haven't talked to them about why Jace doesn't want to come home. I figured you'd want to be part of it."

"Thank you, Jason."

He nodded. They filed into the living room where Summer and Junior awaited them.

"Mommy and I love you, but—"

"Are y'all breakin' up?" Summer shrieked.

"Yes, baby," Destiny responded. It broke her heart to have this conversation with her young teen. But in a way, she was relieved. She never wanted Summer to believe it was okay for a man to treat her the way Jason was with Destiny in their marriage.

"Where we gonna live?" Junior asked.

Destiny peered over at Jason whose thumbnail was lodged in his mouth.

"I'm going to stay with grandma until I can find an apartment."

"But where we gonna live? Do I gotta get a new room?"

"Nobody cares about your room. What happened? I mean, I know y'all weren't close, but he didn't hit you, right?" Summer pressed.

Destiny loved her children. Summer acted more mature than she had to because of the girls she surrounded herself with. She was simply parroting what entertainers talked about online.

"I didn't hit your mom. But I wasn't nice to mommy's heart. We aren't going to be a couple, but we are still going to raise you together."

"How you gonna raise us from Grandma's?" Junior asked. He was more curious than upset. Summer, on the other hand, was as tight as her big brother.

"Grandma says you can stay over with me as much as you like," Jason added.

"Yay!" Junior scurried from the room like the conversation was over.

"What are you thinkin', baby girl?" Destiny asked.

"How was he mean to your heart?" A tear streamed down her round face. She was her father's twin.

"This is hard for me to admit, Summer, but I cheated on Mommy."

Summer's mouth fell open. "Why?"

Tears stung Destiny's eyes. She couldn't protect her children from this hurt. She was a failure. If she could trade places with her daughter at this moment, she would.

"I don't know how to answer that. I don't have an excuse, but she doesn't deserve cheating, and neither do you."

"Can I stay at Grandpa's with Jace?"

Junior reentered the living room with his colorful suitcase and bookbag. "I don't want to go to Grandpa's. He mean. I'm going to Grandma's with Dad."

Destiny felt like someone slapped her. Why was everyone in a hurry to get away? It was one thing for Jace to take some space, but now all the kids wanted sleepovers?

"Nobody said anything about the two of you going. I'm leaving until I get a new place, then you two will live between this house and mine."

"Mom, please!" Junior whined.

She looked to Jason who sort of shrugged. "Give me a second to speak to Mommy in the kitchen."

"This is your call. My parents are a hot ass mess when they're together, but separately, they do well with the kids."

"Like us?" Destiny had a migraine from the number of tears she'd cried in the past forty-eight hours. The thought that they'd recreated how he grew up was unsettling. Jason's parents took most of his lifetime to realize they were better parents when they weren't a couple. He told Destiny how unstable it was for him when they did their back and forth, on again-off again dance.

Jason poked her under the neck which made her head fall to her chest reflexively. In the beginning of their relationship, he made her laugh, and it was exactly what she needed at that point in her life.

"Are you going to be OK with everyone out of the house?"

Destiny stared off in the direction of their family photo. She would be okay, but she wouldn't get a wink of sleep worrying how everything would turn out.

"Have you ever stayed overnight at the house by yourself?"

"There were times you were gone, but the kids were still here. I'd rather they be fine. If your dad is OK with Summer and Jace there, and your mom is good with you and Junior there, it works for me."

Jason gave her a faint smile and lifted his hand for a high-five.

Had cheating lost its allure now that he didn't have to sneak around? Some of the women he slept with were also married.

Jason and Junior left first. She gave him the biggest hug she could. Her son would return the next day, but when he did, nothing would be the same. Summer got picked up by Jason's dad.

When her father-in-law pulled into the driveway, she saw Jace was in the front seat. She knocked on the window while Summer got in.

"Step out for a second," Destiny said. Her voice was low enough for the two of them to hear.

Jace lifted from his seat. They stared at each other because she didn't know what to say.

"I'm sorry."

"I know, Ma." Jace leaned down and hugged her. When he tried to pull away, she wouldn't let him.

A chuckle escaped his lips. "OK. Enough, Mom."

"Can we talk tomorrow? Just me and you?"

Jace nodded and leaned in to kiss her on the cheek.

She watched as the car backed out of the driveway. Realization slammed into her. Destiny was alone. She had no earthly idea how she would make it through the night.

Zay J was upset by the news his parents relayed to him when he got home from school.

He decided they would wait to tell him about Jace. Once Simone said she wasn't staying in the house, it took them almost an hour to convince him she would come back and pick him up in the morning to take him to school. Zay J was the first to remind them that his mom hated Tinsville.

Xavier regretted telling the truth, but Simone insisted they rip the bandage off as far as pretending to be together any longer or sleeping in different rooms. Once Zay J was in the shower for the night,

Simone reminded Xavier that, eventually, she may want to move, but she would be patient and move at a pace that worked best for their son.

Simone left the house with Jeff for the night. If he wasn't trying to meet Xavier Jr. or disrespect his house, Xavier didn't care. He watched from his kitchen window, as a second car left Destiny's driveway with his son and her daughter. Jason and their son left moments before. Destiny was at the house alone.

He knocked on Zay J's door to find him under the covers, barely awake.

"I told you I'm good, Dad. Just sleepy."

"OK. I might step outside for a second. Call me if you need me."

Zay nodded and refocused on his small television screen. Xavier stepped into his room and pinched his cheek. "I love you, Zay J."

"I love you tooooo," he said. Irritation dripped from his words. All he wanted was to get back to his favorite show.

Xavier closed the door quietly behind him and made a beeline for the shower. The excitement that coursed through his veins was unfamiliar. He hadn't been this giddy about a woman in years. Xavier showered in record time. He stepped into a pair of sweats and a T-shirt and peeked in on Zay J one last time.

He'd fallen asleep, so Xavier clicked off his TV. He would be out like a light until morning. Xavier still picked up his phone and checked to ensure he had sufficient battery in case he needed to call. When he did, he saw messages between him and Simone. Simone said she'd be back whenever he texted or called.

Xavier locked his son in and armed the alarm. He looked up and down the street and saw no one. There was still a possibility that someone would see him. He genuinely couldn't care less. With impossibly long strides, he was in front of Destiny's door in seconds.

Xavier: *Let me in*

Dee Dee: *shocked emoji *Am I supposed to know what this means*

Xavier: *It means I'm at the door. Let me in. Didn't want to scare you with a knock*

Footsteps approached the door. They matched the pace of his heart and his breath. The door cracked open, and wide eyes stared up at him. A slow smile spread across Xavier's face. He didn't give a damn what happened before or what would happen tomorrow. He would enjoy his time with Destiny in whatever manner she allowed.

She opened the door wider, and he almost stumbled when he saw what she wore. She may have been the woman he never forgot, but when he left, Destiny was a girl. She closed the door behind him, and when she did, he saw the backside of a grown ass woman.

Xavier would relearn her. What she liked. What she didn't like. What made her moan. He adjusted his sweats but was sure she'd seen the evidence of his excitement. The mahogany tint of her skin against the blush pink negligee she wore had him at attention.

"What are you doing here?"

"What are you wearing?" Xavier hadn't tried to play it cool. He stared at her because he wanted to memorize every moment of their time without the distraction of children or exes. "Is this from the store I found you at?"

"Yes."

"Do you always dress like this?" Xavier's jealousy bubbled to the surface. Coop didn't deserve her.

"Please. I haven't had sex in over a year." Destiny covered her mouth with a closed fist. She wore a blush on her brown cheeks when she looked away.

Xavier was relieved and pissed at once. Cooper had a beautifully built woman, and he hadn't slept with her. *What a fuckin' idiot.*

"I can help you with that."

Destiny peered up at Xavier. Without hesitation, she stepped forward and pressed her lips against his. He willingly accepted her. The thin, sheer fabric of her nighty made his head spin. Soft lips connected with his. Xavier hadn't gone a year without sex, but he'd gone eighteen without her.

When she leaned back for air, he pulled her into him for an embrace. They stood with her in his arms hugging for what felt like an eternity. He was powerless to protect her from all she must have gone through in her marriage and raising their son without him. Xavier was still upset whenever he thought about the time he lost with Jace, but once he learned what she was up against, he understood why she may have made such a terrible decision.

"You still want me, Dee Dee?"

Destiny lifted her head and nodded. Xavier internally counted to ten. He spent too many nights ashamed of himself about the fantasies he still had about her after all this time. He backed her into the island, between her living room and kitchen, and pinned her between his hands. With his hands rested on either side of her, he lowered his head to her neck.

He nibbled and licked her sensitive flesh and let her whimpers serenade his ears. Destiny leaned back and rested her elbows on the counter. Xavier watched the easy way her titties bounced with each of her movements. She smirked at him, and he could have shot off in his pants if he wasn't careful. Xavier leaned back in, and this time when their mouths connected, he slipped his hands down her shorts.

Destiny was bare underneath because he noted the unrestricted sway of her cheeks when she closed the door behind him. But nothing could have prepared him for her juicy ass in his hands. Destiny had glowed up. She always had curves that put him in a trance, but now they'd filled out.

He moved his mouth long enough to say, "Shit, girl."

Destiny's hand against his jawline caused a groan to rumble deep in his throat. She still had that damn smirk on her face, and he had a few ideas of how he could wipe it off. He snatched her shorts down and stared at her neatly groomed pussy. Xavier had seen his share of naked women, but what had been missing was the invisible connection like the one he shared with Destiny.

She was the sexiest woman he'd ever seen. Not perfect by any means, but perfect for him. His hand found her center, and her eyes drifted close.

"Look at me, baby."

Destiny's brows furrowed, but she finally did as he asked.

"I want you to enjoy me. Don't go anywhere else in your head or worry about shit else but us tonight. OK?"

She tucked her bottom lip between her teeth. He hadn't removed his hand. In fact, he lightly stroked her pearl with the pad of his thumb while he spoke. The smirk was gone from her face.

"OK."

Xavier lifted her from her rested position on her elbows and removed the flimsy shirt she wore. *Coop must be a fool to let a woman this fine go without.* He ran his hands up and down her arms and placed sensual kisses on her shoulders. Destiny pulled his face to her and devoured his mouth. In the past, she let him take the lead; things had changed. She led him backward until his thighs bumped the side of the couch.

She pushed him so he was seated and straddled his lap. *Damn!*

Xavier's mouth found her darkened nipples and latched on like his life depended on it. Destiny's moans were louder, and her hips grinded in his lap.

"Slow down, baby." Xavier wanted to savor every moment with her.

"I can't. I want you inside me, Zay."

Something inside of him snapped. He lifted his ass and pulled his boxers and sweats down in one motion. Destiny barely let him remove his shirt before she lowered her warmth near his shaft. The proximity of their anatomy had each of them on the brink of release.

"Shit!"

She wrapped her arms around his neck and licked the side of his ear. Destiny grinded against him as if she didn't need his participation whatsoever. Xavier threw his head back in ecstasy. His hands gripped her ass, and her center get juicer.

He berated himself. He should have held out and tasted her first, but he was too far gone. His highest priority was to get inside of Destiny.

"Zay!"

He snapped out of the trance her pussy put him in and stood with her in his arms. He hadn't taken the time to get a tour of her place, but he saw a nearby blanket and laid it across the floor.

"Can I use this?"

She nodded.

Xavier placed her on the floor and stroked his dick while he regarded her.

"Play with it, Dee Dee. Show me how you like to be touched."

Destiny placed one hand between her legs while the other pinched her nipple. She maintained eye contact with him as she slid her fingers in and out of her slick center. Her mouth was open, but no sound came out—her lips were in a constant 'O' shape.

"I'm jealous of your hands."

There was the smirk that he liked. Xavier took in her velvety skin. She smelled like oranges and roses. Maybe she'd just had a bath.

"I was pretending it was you like I always do."

Xavier had enough of watching the show. He lowered himself to enter her. If he had any doubt she hadn't had sex in months, her tightness confirmed her admission.

"It's so tight."

He struggled to get inside of her, despite how wet she was.

"Let me in. Please, baby. Let me in."

Destiny relaxed enough for him to enter, and he swore he blacked out for a few seconds. The bottom of his balls tingled the moment he was inside.

"Zay!"

"Yeah, baby."

Destiny pulled him closer to her and continued to whisper freaky shit in his ear. "I fantasize about you all the time. I imagined what you would look and feel like now that you're older."

Xavier pulled back and found her eyes. "And?"

"You feel better." She bit the bottom of his earlobe and wrapped her legs around him.

"Shit!"

Xavier's strokes were slow, deep, and measured. He'd fantasized about her too, and just as she admitted, she felt much better than any dream ever could. Her legs shook, and she released his ear from her lips. Her mouth hung open as an orgasm tore through her body. He watched every wrinkle between her brows as if it was necessary for him to commit her fuck faces to memory.

When she opened her eyes, they were full of tears.

"Did I hurt you, baby?" Xavier stilled and awaited her answer.

"No. Please don't stop," she whined.

"Destiny, what's wrong?"

"I'm sorry."

He leaned in and kissed her softly around her mouth. He kissed her tears and rubbed his hand across her natural hair. "I know."

Her body shook from an emotion unrelated to sexual pleasure.

"Baby."

"It's so good. I don't deserve you," Destiny added.

"Yeah, maybe you don't." Xavier was playful in his tone as he continued his movement. "Can I take my frustration out on your pussy?"

Destiny's eyes rolled back, and her pussy get wetter. He was impressed with how well her body responded to his words.

"I said, you gon' let me take my grievances out on this pussy?" Xavier increased the pace of his strokes to emphasize his words. But when she didn't respond, he stilled.

Her eyes popped open. "You can do whatever you want with your pussy."

Xavier hummed his delight. It took everything he had to hold back his release. *His pussy?*

"Don't be playin' with me."

"My pussy has belonged to you since the first time you entered me, Zay."

He tucked his bottom lip between his teeth. "I can punish it if I want to?"

"Yep."

"Turn your ass around. I'mma need to hit this shit from the back."

Destiny's eyes bulged. He remembered how nervous she was to let him get behind her when they were younger because she said he always went too deep. That was too damn bad because he was about to put in work.

She lifted, and once again, the sight of her body had the bottom of his balls ready to pop off. He stared down at her and rubbed her ass cheeks. He pulled them apart and put his face between them to eat her pussy from the back. Destiny yelped, and her body contracted. She had her second orgasm, and he wasn't even inside of her. She tried to lay on her stomach.

He wiped his face and slapped her ass. "Hell nah. On your knees, so you can take this punishment."

She lifted herself, and he entered her fiercely. "Zay!"

He pounded her cheeks like she deserved. The bounce back of Destiny's ass tempted and urged him to continue. Her moans let him know she enjoyed her punishment as much as he savored giving it to her.

"You kept my family from me."

"I'm sorry, baby."

"You kept this good ass pussy from me!" He plowed into her and accented each of his grips with deep thrusts.

"I'm sorry, baby." Her body stiffened like she was on the verge of another orgasm, but Xavier stilled.

She craned her neck to look back at him. His brows were bunched together, and his breaths were ragged. He didn't want to stop, but she needed to be taught a lesson. And if it was his pussy to do as he pleased, she wouldn't get her release until he said she could.

"Please."

Destiny tightened her muscles around him. He began his movement because he felt like she put a spell on him.

"Destiny, shit!"

She wiggled and bounced her ass and had his head spinning. Destiny tooted her ass up and leaned down to rest on her elbows. The sight of her face down and ass up made his toes curl.

He rammed into her repeatedly. He was supposed to hold out, but the pussy was too good.

"Cum with me, Dee Dee."

Her body tensed at the sound of his words, and he swore his nut was so strong he went blind for a few seconds. She lowered herself to the floor completely, and he followed, still buried inside of her.

"Shit, I love you," Xavier said on an exhale. Destiny's light snores tickled his ears. He slapped her ass. "You hear me?"

"Yeah, Zay. I love you too."

Chapter Six

Destiny peeled her eyes open, certain she'd been engulfed in another life like fantasy with Xavier Grant. She wasn't in her room. The warmth from the body next to hers made it unnecessary for her duvet that was usually wrapped around her body twice because she slept alone. Jason rarely slept in the bed with her. When he did, he was never this close.

She lifted, and realization of the night's events fluttered through her mind.

"Zay?"

His heavy arm barely moved when she lifted. Xavier Grant was here. And they slept together last night. Twice. A blush covered her cheeks as she remembered all they did.

Destiny studied his face. She was crazy about Xavier, whether she could see those hazel eyes or not. She'd be a flat-out liar if she pretended she wasn't attracted to the color of his eyes, but unlike many of the other women in their town, Destiny was tempted by the entire man. He hadn't bothered to put his shirt back on. His muscular chest taunted her with another good time if only she was willing to surrender to her desires.

Her gaze fell below the happy trail of dusty brown hair that traveled from his navel to the patch of heaven she had yet to bury her face in. Xavier was naked. Although the sun wasn't fully awake, his manhood was. She looked up to find his eyes on her. He'd caught her mid-stare.

"Come here," he said with a scratchy, hypnotic voice that had to be against the law.

She slid her eyes to the wall clock to see it was almost five a.m. They would have a few hours before they needed to face the day. Xavier tugged on her until she leaned over him. He looked at her like he hadn't just had her a few hours ago.

Xavier's stamina was unmatched. When they were teenagers, they had sex so many times in one weekend the skin on his dick chaffed. Destiny had redressed in her nighty set last night, for fear she would get too cold. He easily pulled the top over her head and adjusted her position to take off her small shorts.

He was ready for round three. Her mind wanted to protest. It was necessary for them to talk. They still had too many loose ends.

"Come here, baby," he repeated.

"I'm right here."

"No, you're not. You went somewhere else in your head."

Destiny hung her head. She was naked, but with Xavier, she was more vulnerable than she was in her nearly twenty-year marriage.

"I don't know how things went with you and Coop, but I want you right here with me, body, mind, and soul." He tilted her chin up. "I don't want to make love to you while you're busy in your head."

Why did he have to speak to her like that? What the hell would they do after today? They were both married to other people. Xavier, in person, with his hands and lips on her, was a recipe for disaster. There was no way she wouldn't want this treatment every day, and that wasn't going to happen.

"Don't leave me by myself, Dee Dee."

She stared at him, then let her gaze fall to his lips. They perked up. He adjusted her so she sat on his lap with her knees on the outside of his taut thighs.

"Can I have you again, baby?"

His lips were against her ear when he spoke. Sensations of pure pleasure ran the length of her spine. A gush of her essence release in his lap.

"Yes."

Xavier grabbed his length and lined it up with her split. Destiny's head was thrown back when Xavier pulled her down on him. She cried out. Her body still hadn't adjusted to the girth Xavier was blessed with. Despite her wetness, she remained a snug fit.

With her head thrown back, Xavier planted kisses on her neck. His nibbles and licks made her body contort in satisfaction. His hands caressed her back softly. Destiny was convinced he was a magician and that maybe she was a lazy lover. He used his hips to thrust up into her, his mouth on the sensitive part of her neck, and his hands to stimulate the flesh of her arms and back.

"I love this shit!"

Destiny hummed her agreement.

"And I love you, Dee Dee."

Water filled Destiny's eyes as they always seemed to when she was near him. And right on cue, Xavier lips connected above her cheeks to kiss her tears away.

"You love me, baby?" Xavier inspected Destiny closely to search for any hesitation on her part.

She nodded as tears continued to fall from her eyes. How the hell had she made such a mess of her life. She was in love with a married man. He insisted his wife didn't believe in marriage, but they had children—young children who would likely see her as a homewrecker.

"Tell me you love me."

"I love you, Zay."

Xavier repositioned them so that she was flat on her back. He leaned in and wrapped her legs around his back. His strokes were deep and unhurried.

"Open up for me."

Destiny got wetter each time he told her what he wanted. Nothing turned her on more. She lifted her legs and held them at the ankles. If he wanted open, he could have it. Xavier Grant could have it all.

"Damn, girl."

Xavier put his hand between them and pushed on her bud. It was all it took for her to completely unravel. She cried out until she could barely feel her legs. Xavier shifted one over his shoulder. He kissed it and gazed in her eyes as he continued his pleasurable assault.

Destiny leaned up and bit the bottom of Xavier's ear. It drove him crazy when she put her lips on his ear. She licked the outside for good measure. His thrusts became chaotic until he found his release. He roared her name and leaned to the side, so they were faced toward each other still connected.

They drifted back to sleep. The piercing sound of the trash truck yanked Destiny from her restful, satiated sleep.

"Xavier. It's almost seven."

Xavier stood. How this man still had a hard dick was beyond her. He grabbed his boxers and sweats and shuffled for his phone.

"Zay J hasn't called me yet, but he'll be up looking for breakfast soon."

He leaned down and sprinkled kisses on her cheek and along her jawline.

"Call me later."

An emptiness hung in the air. She wouldn't call him. She needed to sort shit out, and there was no way she could do that with the thumps between her legs she got whenever she thought of him.

"Hey."

She lifted her head to face him. She hadn't bothered with clothes. The kids packed clothes for school when they left for their grandparents, but she did want Xavier out before her neighbors woke up.

"You're overthinking this, baby."

"Am I?"

Xavier crouched down to her level and grabbed her chin.

"There's a lot that we have to do. I'm not naive to think every day can be like it was last night. But I'm a patient man."

Destiny gave him a weak smile.

"But know this, I don't regret what we did or how quickly we moved."

She did.

"Walk me to the door, Double D."

He pulled her to stand and draped a blanket over her arms.

"As sexy as you look right now, I gotta cover you up. I'd scratch somebody's eyes out if they saw all this."

Destiny's cheeks flushed. Jason was never territorial with her. It was as though he couldn't care less who saw her or paid her extra attention. A guy flirted with her while she and the family were at the mall, and Jason didn't bat an eye. Destiny closed the blanket around her and wobbled toward the door. She was sore from their rough lovemaking.

"You not gonna ghost me, are you?"

There was an expression on his handsome face she couldn't place. He'd asked jokingly, but Xavier's eyes couldn't lie. They also saw through her. She had no intentions to call him back. There were too many other things that required her undivided attention—like Jace.

She shook her head. Xavier tipped her chin up and kissed her like they may never kiss again. Destiny wasn't convinced they would.

After Xavier left, Destiny took the time to straighten up her home. She opened the windows to invite fresh air in. Her home smelled like the result of her lovemaking with Zay. Xavier Grant was back, and he loved her. No matter how complicated her life was, he didn't seem the least bit deterred.

Destiny showered and dressed for work as flashes of the night before drifted through her mind. It was the way he spoke to her and the rough sound of his voice when he did that had her knees weak even now. She drove to work on autopilot. Between pleasant memories of her time with Xavier were gut-wrenching reminders of her first-born's disappointment. Destiny fought the urge to remind him that they were supposed to talk later today.

Maybe she would pick him up for lunch. It was a ritual they did often when he was in elementary and junior high. Initially, she did it because he complained about the length of time he was away from her during the day. But once she had Summer and Junior, it had been Destiny's way of making sure Jace didn't feel less special because he was no longer the baby.

She sat in her car for at least twenty minutes, delaying the inevitable. Her *Upundies* location was to have several visiting managers shadow her store to determine which practices might improve sales at their branch. That meant Ivory would be there. She'd sent her an email and included their boss, asking what she should bring. *Bitch! Bring a videographer for all I care. Kissing up ain't gon' help you sell more panties.*

Destiny arrived at her store an hour before the other managers were to arrive. Yet the first face she saw was Ivory's. Destiny couldn't wrap her mind around how someone this perfect could be jealous of her. Ivory had money. She didn't need to work at a lingerie store.

Her body was beautiful, and she could easily model for the *Upundies* campaigns if she wanted. Destiny was an unhappy wife and mother of three amazing children. Every day seemed to blend and drag painfully slow. The only time she was fulfilled was when she was with her kids. Although she was in her head, overthinking her entire life choices and where they would lead her, she had to admit she had a glow about her today.

She hadn't recognized herself when she saw her reflection in the mirror. Her skin was luminous, and her eyes no longer only held the sadness they'd held for years. There was hope there, and Xavier Grant was the catalyst for her radiance. The smirk she wore when he saw her naked hadn't left her lips.

"Somebody's in a good mood," Ivory said, interrupting Destiny's daydream.

"Hey, Ivory. You're early." Destiny spoke through gritted teeth and mirrored Ivory's insincere smile.

"I didn't want to wait for the others. I need to know exactly what you do if I'm going to be like you when I grow up."

One of Destiny's employees, Renee, choked on her coffee when Ivory spoke. Renee had confided in Destiny that she found out she was pregnant. She had convinced herself Destiny would be disappointed and cut her hours since she'd just graduated from high school. To her surprise, Destiny shared how she'd had a baby when she started with the company, and after she graduated with her associates, *Upundies* promoted her and gave her the flexibility necessary for a working mother.

One of Destiny's favorite things about Renee was her intolerance for bullshit. Unlike her boss, Renee didn't shy away from confrontation. She called a spade a spade. And while there was space for both of their strengths, Destiny had a good feeling about Renee's promise and ability to hold management positions if that was what she desired.

Destiny still hadn't gotten the chance to put her bag away. Her cell phone buzzed, and she rumbled for it while she spoke to Renee.

Xavier Grant: *I don't have to start work until Monday*

Destiny's eyes lit up.

Destiny: *Why are you telling me this?*

Xavier Grant: *I think you know*

Destiny: *I don't want wet panties at work*

Xavier Grant: *Take them off*

"Is this how a newly appointed district manager starts their day? Flirting with their husband?" Ivory's tone was dry, and she rolled her eyes when she said husband.

Ivory was of the same mind as Simone. If Xavier was honest about his current wife's outlook on marriage, both she and Ivory didn't agree with the institution. Ivory expressed countless times how antiquated marriage was. She insisted that a lurid affair was all she ever wanted.

"Actually, no." Because she wasn't texting Jason. Destiny smirked to herself as she walked to the back to put her things away and continue flirting with Zay.

Destiny: *I just got to work. I need to focus*

Xavier Grant: *Do you like dick pics*

Destiny: *Zay!!!*

She laughed out loud as she placed her bag in a cubby in the employee locker room.

Xavier Grant: *Good, you need to laugh*

Destiny whipped around. Was he in the store?

Xavier Grant: *I can't see you, but I want to*

Destiny: *Wish I could. Today will be stressful. I have to train some catty women on how to sell more of those nighties you enjoyed so much*

Xavier Grant: *Damn*

Destiny smiled as she could only imagine where his mind had gone.

Destiny: *I really have to go. Later*

Xavier Grant: *OK, love you*

Destiny silenced her phone. Why did he have to text her like that? She didn't deserve a happily ever after. She did the unforgivable. What if Jace didn't want a relationship with him? Would he love her then? What if Simone changed her mind about marriage? Maybe she didn't believe in marriage, but after twelve years and talks of divorce, she could change her mind.

Destiny was determined to use work as a distraction to questions her brain couldn't possibly answer. All she had to do was make it to lunch. Then she could shift her focus to her son. He mattered. Their relationship was her priority.

Customers came in spurts, and Destiny's team handled them with ease. One of the midday rushes required all hands-on deck, and Destiny noticed Ivory watch the way she and her girls handled hiccups. She had to give it to her; while other managers jumped in to help, Ivory took mental notes. She hadn't let customers distract her from her reason for her visit. Ivory had even asked Destiny several questions on why she chose a specific course of action over another.

Once the shoppers dwindled, Ivory was bored, and her inner bitch piped up.

"How do you live in this dinky ass town? I would shoot myself just to stay entertained."

"Let me know if you need any help," Destiny said with her head buried in transaction receipts from the previous week.

"Ha ha," she started. Ivory was behind the desk with Destiny. She lifted abruptly and caused a few papers to fall when she did. "Who in the entire fuck is that?" She added dramatic pauses between each of her words which earned her a chuckle from Destiny. "I'm usually into deep chocolate men with full beards, but I'll make an exception. You didn't tell me Tinsville had a clean-cut gem like him."

Destiny hadn't bothered to see who Ivory went on about. There were attractive men in Tinsville, but she was used to them. There was only one man who could illicit the energy Ivory was on.

"How do I look? He's headed our way?"

Destiny peered up at Ivory. "You a'ight. If he's into the long legs, model type, you're in there."

"I'm into the short, curvy, natural hair type."

Destiny stilled. Ivory slapped her arm to get her attention, but Destiny didn't have to look up to know Xavier was in front of her counter. She recognized that voice anywhere.

"Can I borrow you for a minute?"

Destiny finally gazed up. Those hazel eyes pierced any sense of self-control she had. The thumps between her legs were stronger than an HBCU drumline. She nodded.

"Destiny Cooper! You know this man?" Ivory all but yelled.

Xavier's jaw tightened. She could only imagine how difficult it was for him to hear her name associated with Jason's. Destiny was overcome with jealousy at the idea that Simone had Xavier's last name. Destiny's eyes swung to Ivory, and a wide grin spread across her face.

"Me and Renee will take care of things for as long as you need, you lucky bitch."

Destiny rounded the corner on wobbly legs. He didn't kiss her or hug her, but his physical proximity to her body likely made their familiarity obvious.

"What are you doing here?" she asked as she craned her neck up to see him.

"I don't know."

"Where are we going?"

"I don't know, baby." He led her into a hallway between department stores and glared down at her.

"What's wrong?"

"We're in a bubble right now."

"Zay, what are you talking about?"

"I mean once I meet my son and the kids transition from their normal routines, shit might hit the fan."

Destiny lowered her head, and her shoulders slumped. She'd already prepared herself for this. It was the reason she had no intention of calling Zay after he left her house this morning.

"I needed to see you before all of that."

Xavier's breathing increased. He had the look in his eye that ruined her panties. Destiny swallowed. This was lust, not love. They shouldn't take it there again, at least not now.

"You've seen me. I should get back." She swallowed hard as he inched closer to her.

Destiny stole a glance around her, and although the mall was rather empty, they were not in a private space. When she returned her gaze to Xavier, he lowered his head and latched on to her mouth. He pushed his hands down the back of her fitted skirt. How he could fit his large hands down her clothes was always a mystery to her.

She returned his kiss and melted when his hands rubbed against her flesh. A couple's conversation alerted her that they were not alone. She separated from him before they passed the opened hallway.

"We shouldn't do this."

"Why not?" Xavier asked with total sincerity laced in his words.

Destiny's chest heaved. She was confused and aroused. "Because you said it yourself. We're in a bubble. We don't know what's going to happen with Jace or our other children. What if Jace hates you? What if Simone changes her mind about staying with you?"

Xavier chuckled.

"What the hell is so funny?"

"She doesn't want me. She's with Jeff."

"Who the hell is Jeff?"

"The man I caught her in my house with when I came home to ask for an official separation. She stayed with him last night."

Destiny's mind reeled as she attempted to keep up with him. Her hand flew to her heart. "Xavier Jr. was alone last night?"

Xavier met her concerned look with a half grin.

"Zay, I'm being serious."

"I know, and it's cute. He was alone, but he had his phone, and I locked him in."

"This is what I mean. Neither of us is being rational. Anything could have happened."

"I was across the damn street." Xavier ran a hand down his neatly groomed goatee, the one with the stubble that scratched her thighs when he ate her from the back. "I'm glad you're concerned about Zay J."

"I like his nickname. It's cute."

"His mom hates it."

Destiny blew out a breath. "I need to get back to work." She tried to turn away from him, but his long arms brought her back.

"I'm not going to stand here and lie; I want to fuck you bad. But that's not all this is for me, Dee Dee."

She wouldn't look at him, so he lifted her chin up to him.

"I love you, and I meant it."

"But—"

"It's not going to change if Jace hates me."

"What if Simone wants half? What if she makes your divorce unnecessarily painful? Where does that leave Zay J?"

"I'll give it to her. I'm not hurting for money, Destiny. And if she makes the divorce painful, I'll deal with it. None of that will change the way I feel about you."

"Are you still mad at me for not telling you?"

Xavier's jaw tightened again. "Yes. Sometimes I am."

Destiny dipped her head again. He should be pissed at her. She was so fearful to rock the boat that she didn't do what it took to tell Jace and Xavier the truth. She didn't deserve his forgiveness, but she prayed like hell she could make things right with her son.

"But that's life, baby. If I can forgive Willie Earl, I can forgive you."

He lifted her chin again and pulled her in for an unhurried kiss.

"Plus, you said this pussy belongs to me." He peeked around to make sure no one was near them and walked her to a dark part of the hallway. He placed his hand under her skirt and slipped past her soggy underwear. "Damn, girl. Is it always this wet?"

Destiny blushed. "No."

He stroked her center and leaned in to whisper beside her ear. "If I get mad, I'll just take it out on this pussy."

Destiny's eyes rolled back. She was on the verge of release from Xavier's words and finger when Ivory's voice interrupted them.

"Destiny? I have a quick question for you?"

"Shit," Destiny groaned.

Xavier smoothed her skirt for her and let out a quiet chuckle. "Is she one of the catty women making your day stressful?"

Destiny rolled her eyes playfully. "She hasn't been too bad today. She has a crush on you though."

Ivory rounded the corner. "Oh. It can wait. I'll see you back inside." She winked at Xavier and headed back for the store.

"I need to go."

"I know. I'll walk you."

They walked the short distance in silence. Once they reached the entryway, Destiny said, "I'm going to pick up Jace for lunch to talk."

"Good luck. Would you tell me how it goes?"

"Of course. Bye, Zay."

Xavier pinched her cheek in lieu of the kiss she wanted but accepted they shouldn't share. "Bye, Dee Dee."

* * *

Tinsville Heights High School wasn't the same as when she was a student. Everything was bright and shiny. The building had been reconstructed almost a decade ago in comparison to the forty-year-old building Destiny remembered. She hadn't called or texted ahead and figured this could either work in her favor or blow up in her face.

"Hi. I'm here to sign out Jace Cooper," Destiny said to the receptionist.

"Jace Cooper. Is he Coop's son?" The slightly familiar woman's eyes were wide when she spoke.

You gotta be fuckin' kidding me. Please tell me he did not sleep with somebody from Jace's school.

"He is."

She handed the slip of paper to the student worker and returned her attention to Destiny.

"Tell him Sherry says hello."

"Tell him yourself." Destiny took the seat across from the glass office. She didn't give a damn that Jason had slept with most of Tinsville, but the nerve of some of the women was beyond disrespectful. *Bitch!*

She didn't bother to look at the woman again.

"Mom? What's wrong?" Jace's voice broke into Destiny's rapid thoughts. He was scared.

She stood and approached him. "No. Nothing is wrong. I'm sorry I scared you."

81

He threw his head back as relief washed over him. Jace was tall and handsome. It was hard for her to see him as a young man and not just her baby boy.

"What are you doing here then?"

Eyes were on them, so she led him toward the entrance. "I signed you out of school for the rest of the day. I wanted to take you to lunch... only if you want."

Jace's innocent smile covered his youthful features.

"What?" Destiny was relieved but confused at his amusement.

"You going to drive to my dorm and try to take me to lunch?"

"If I have to."

"Yeah, Ma. Let's go to lunch."

Chapter Seven

Donald invited Xavier out for drinks Friday evening. He was glad for the distraction. Simone had an extended hotel in the nicer suburban town ten minutes from Tinsville, and she had Zay J for the weekend. If he couldn't be with Destiny or Zay J and he didn't officially start work until Monday, he'd climb the walls from boredom.

"Grant! Your body finally caught up with your head." Donald was Xavier's former basketball coach and referred to him by his last name.

Coach Donald Archer was a Tinsville Heights treasure. He was responsible for fathering many of the city's black youth. He taught black boys how to be men when the only other people available were the OGs and the police. While Xavier would never turn his nose up at the street disciples, their brotherhood came at a price he wasn't willing to pay. His long legs gave him basketball as an alternative.

Xavier had no doubt that if he wasn't as talented at ball as he was, his misguided anger would have landed him in jail or worse. Coach Archer taught him to channel his power or be overtaken by it.

Through the years, they kept in touch. He always asked when Xavier would give back some of what he was given in Tinsville.

Xavier had no intentions of returning to his hometown, but Archer wore him down, especially when he told him about the soon-to-be vacant CFO position with the Tinsville City Schools. Because of the positive impact Donald Archer had on the area, his recommendation held more weight than all the experience in the world. The hiring committee made it clear that it was the main reason he got the job. He had six months to prove Archer right.

"Coach Archer, you look older. I didn't think that was possible."

Xavier leaned in and gave his mentor a tight hug.

"Let me go. You damn kids hug too tight. I told my son the same thing. You know this fool had the nerve to lift me off my feet." Donald's dry laugh echoed off the walls of the quiet lounge.

"We love you big, old man."

"Yeah, whatever."

Xavier took a seat and looked around. "Where the hell you got me, Coach?"

"Can you please call me Donald?"

"No, sir. That would be disrespectful. Like calling my grandpa by his first name," Xavier said through a chuckle.

"You got one more damn time to call me old. Wait 'til your kid grows up. He probably already thinks your ass is old."

"The other day, we were tossing the football and he said I'm old because I was born in the nineteens."

Archer's laughter boomed.

"Exactly. I'm already being called old."

A young waitress collected their drink orders and menus. Xavier's mind drifted to his boys at the mention of Zay J.

"Get it off your mind, son."

Xavier peered over to see Archer's curious eyes. Destiny was the reason Xavier never wanted to come home.

"I got a kid."

"I know that. Lanky tween like his daddy. He's cuter than you were though."

"I have an eighteen-year-old-son with Destiny Davis."

Archer furrowed his brows in contemplation. "Coop's wife?"

Xavier's jaw tightened. "Yeah."

Archer rubbed his weathered pointer finger under his nose like he did when he was in deep thought. "They got three kids together. Wait. Jace Cooper?"

How petty would it be if I got his name legally changed. Fuckin' Coop.

"Yep."

"You didn't know?"

"No!"

"OK, shit. I'm trying to keep up. Tell me what happened."

"The shortened version is I moved back for the job and happened to move on her street. I wasn't the only one who didn't know. The kid came out when I was talking to Destiny, and he knew immediately. I thought he was just on some teenage stuff. Guess he felt like he'd seen a ghost. Turns out, Coop begged Destiny not to tell him."

"What the hell is wrong with him?"

"Hell if I know." Xavier threw back a shot and let the liquid burn the back of his throat when he did.

"You talked to the kid yet?"

"Nope. Destiny spoke with him the other day once he calmed down."

Xavier's phone rang, and he picked it up on the first ring. It was Destiny. He gave his coach a nod and stood to accept the call. When he came back, he had a goofy grin on his face.

"The wife?" Archer asked.

"Not exactly."

Archer stared at him blankly. "You been here for all of one week, and you're already having an affair."

"It's complicated."

"Well, uncomplicate this shit. You're a good guy, Grant, but

Tinsville is smaller than a rat's asshole. You got two boys looking up to you, and a job whose success is influenced by your reputation. It don't make it fair, but these are small town politics."

Xavier tossed several bills on the table that covered both his and his coach's tab. "I know. I gotta go. Let's do this again soon."

"You too damn old to be thinkin' with your dick, Grant."

Xavier smiled at him brightly. Coach Archer wouldn't understand. Destiny was technically a married woman, and technically, he had a wife. He should still be pissed at Destiny, but he wasn't. He wanted her anytime and any way he could have her. And her call let him know he could have her right now.

* * *

The location Destiny shared with him was for a hotel twenty minutes from Tinsville. He had no idea where her rug rats were, and he'd be a damn lie if he pretended to care. Destiny was a lot of things, but a bad mother wasn't one of them. He was confident that if she was away, her kids were safely accounted for.

Suite Seduction was an upscale hotel for business owners who lived outside of Tinsville. Small towns were opportunities for big business. Entrepreneurs set up businesses like dope boys but refused to eat where they shit.

Xavier remembered the name of the hotel from when he was a teen. His high school basketball team passed Suite Seduction on bus rides to away games. The name's double entendre was hilarious. Now his body responded to it with full understanding of its intent. He wanted nothing more than to explore Destiny in one of those rooms.

Dee Dee: *The front desk has a key for you*

Xavier: *Who is this? And what have you done with Destiny?*

Xavier hardened at the turn of events. He was sure he'd have to pursue Destiny until she accepted they belonged together no matter what anyone else thought.

Dee Dee: *She's here and she's waiting for you. Everything okay?*

Xavier: *Hell yeah. It's just after I left your place Tuesday morning, you seemed like you had no plans to hit me up*

Dee Dee: *I didn't. But I changed my mind. Where are you?*

Xavier: *In my car*

Dee Dee: *Give the receptionist your name and head up*

Xavier: *On my way*

Xavier entered the Suite Seduction, hopeful he wouldn't see anyone he recognized. An attractive receptionist greeted him eagerly.

"Welcome to Suite Seduction, where pleasure with your experience is our highest priority. How might I seduce you today?"

He was about to give his name, but the last part of her statement added a rush of adrenaline to his already excited state. "Excuse me?"

"Corporate makes us say it to each guest. You should see me when I have to say it to married couples. I try to make eye contact with the wife, but I'm not always so lucky."

"I can imagine. I'm Xavier Grant."

The younger woman's cheeks tinted. "Oh, yes. This is for you."

She handed him a black key card tucked inside a white envelope with the written room number and a heart drawn beside it.

"Enjoy your stay, Mr. Grant."

Xavier wandered toward the elevator of the lavish establishment. He was so impatient to be with Destiny that when the elevator didn't come down, he found the stairs and took them two at a time. It had only been a few days since he was with her, and already his body craved her like an addiction. Things were hot and heavy with them when they were younger, and it was as though their first night together after eighteen years woke up what had been dormant within him.

Xavier stood to the side of the suite indicated on the card to slow his ragged breath. He rubbed his hand across his low-cut hair, grateful he'd gotten his hair and face groomed the night before. He tapped lightly on the door. When she opened it, Xavier's mouth fell open. Destiny wore an off-white matching lingerie set. The pushup bra had her girls high and perky where they belonged. The lace thong featured straps that hung against her hips and a second set that rested higher on her waist.

She stared at him with a smirk on her face. There was no longer hesitation in her face when she peered up at him.

Xavier shook his head to clear images of a young Destiny. He'd had a vision of her awaiting him when he returned home from a long day of work. How different would things have been had she reached out and found him while he was away at school?

"You OK?" she asked. Her voice soothed his distracted thoughts and brought him back to the present.

"Yeah."

"Come in, Zay."

The back of her outfit was sexier than the front. Destiny was small and thick, and as he'd experienced the last time they were together, she filled out quite nicely since high school.

"Do you like it?" Destiny asked as she waved her hand toward the spacious suite.

When she did, Xavier had a vision of her with a rounded belly. His palms perspired and his jaw clenched. He would never have the chance to meet a pregnant Destiny. She carried his child for nine months, and he didn't know. What was her labor like? How was Jace as a baby? When would he get a chance to meet him?

"Zay, are you sure you're okay?" Destiny asked as she walked closer to him with concerned eyes.

"I said yes, Destiny. Shit!"

He hadn't meant to raise his voice, but he also hadn't expected to be filled with anger. He wasn't upset with her the last time they were together. Xavier meant it when he insisted he wouldn't take legal action against Destiny because he didn't want to hurt his chances to connect with his son–the son he didn't know because Destiny and Coop kept him.

Destiny froze. Xavier didn't raise his voice. He'd also never been in this position.

"I'm sorry. I was fine before, but I'm suddenly having a hard time."

Her shoulders sagged, and she reached for a floor-length robe to cover herself with. Why would they make the cover sexier than the lingerie itself? His body and mind were at war. And when Destiny turned toward him, he pictured her with a small child propped on her hip—it looked like Jace as a toddler.

Xavier's stomach churned. His father wasn't there for him when he was small. He'd made peace with Willie Earl and had gotten the apology he waited for his entire life. Nobody understood the pain of the absence of a father like Xavier, but he'd turned around and done the same thing to his son. Jace may have had Coop, but he found out Xavier was his real father. He couldn't step into the role of father as easily as he'd stepped into the role as Destiny's lover.

He ran from the room until he stumbled into a bathroom and unloaded the contents of his food and liquor. What the hell was he supposed to do now?

* * *

Destiny paced the floor of her room at Suite Seduction. She had gone against her better judgment and booked a room to spend a night with Xavier. Tiffany would be in town tomorrow, so a guilt-free night of passion with Xavier was what motivated her to send the kids with Jason and his mother for the night. Auntie Tiffany would be around for the next week or longer, so Friday was the perfect time for the family to do their own thing and come back together Saturday afternoon until she touched down.

But Destiny's salacious plan backfired. Xavier was pissed at her. She saw the pain of betrayal in his eyes. He didn't have to say it. Jason looked at her that way so much, it was clear Xavier was irritated with her from the moment he stepped over the threshold. Maybe she should have let him pursue her. Maybe her attempt at seduction only reminded him of how long she'd kept their son a secret.

She shouldn't have been surprised at how hurt he was. Xavier Grant was the type of man who would have wanted to be part of each of Jace's milestones. Her throat burned. He stepped out of the bathroom, and his lightly bronzed features looked like they'd seen a ghost.

"Do you want to tell me what it is?" Destiny asked as she retrieved water for him.

"I came here with every intention of living out all the fantasies I've had for the past two decades. Monday night barely scratched the surface of what I have in mind for us."

Destiny smiled. She was also aware there was a but coming.

"But when you answered the door, my mind saw you younger. I got pissed because of all the nights we missed when I should have come home to you."

A tear escaped Destiny's cheek, and she berated herself to listen without making the conversation about her hurt feelings. It was the least she could do.

"Then once I was inside and you turned, I saw a vision of you with a pregnant belly. And right before I yelled, you held two-year-old Jace on your hip."

Destiny handed him the water with a shaky hand but said nothing.

"Were you alone for his birth?"

"No." She wouldn't offer that Jason and his family were there unless he asked.

"How was he as a baby?" Xavier's words came out in a harsh whisper.

At the thought of baby Jace, Destiny smiled bright. "He was perfect. I had to check Jace's diaper and remember when he ate last because he never cried."

Xavier stared off toward the opened glass window.

"Do you have pictures?"

Destiny walked over to grab her cellphone and surfed through her pictures until she found her album marked Jace. She handed

Xavier the phone and stepped back to give him space to process the beautiful images of the son he recently learned was his.

"He looks exactly like Zay J did at that age. And me."

Destiny nodded. Her son had a stronger resemblance to his father than her or anyone else in her family. Only once did someone question who Jace looked like. It was an awkward moment where another person chimed in about how different families' skin tones and phenotypes present. She'd known the reason was because he looked like Xavier.

He shifted his body in the chair where he sat to face her fully. Gone was the upset. Xavier was concerned.

"How did your conversation go?"

Shit! Of all the things Destiny dreamed about this night, questions about Jace wasn't one of them. She took a seat on the couch opposite where Xavier sat.

"It went well."

Xavier glared at her.

"But he's not ready to meet you."

A tight line formed Xavier's face. He rubbed the stubble alongside his goatee, then scratched his eyebrow. Destiny held her breath as she awaited his next words. She had a feeling it wouldn't be something she wanted to hear.

"I need a minute," he said.

Xavier had unknowingly hit her with the same words their son did when he learned the truth. Her worst fear was that Jace wouldn't forgive her, but he had. Would his dad be able to extend the same grace? Destiny was clear she didn't deserve it, but her heart and soul wanted Xavier Grant and his forgiveness. She'd do whatever it took to get him back, no matter how long it took.

Chapter Eight

Destiny had too much pride to return home last night. She cried herself to sleep in the humongous bed crafted for the space of at least two lovers. Xavier was done. Her non-disclosure had settled over him to the point where he could barely stand the sight of her. When he left to clear his head, she felt like someone knocked the wind out of her.

It was a rash decision to get a suite simply because Tiffany was on her way to town. Destiny couldn't bear the idea that she'd have to go days without him now that she'd had a taste of the level of passion her body went without for so long. But now, she doubted if Xavier would willingly see her again. As a mother, she supported her son's need to take his time before he met his birth father. She wouldn't force it.

Whether he deserved it or not, Jace was loyal to Jason, who had been in the role of father his entire life. Jace was upset that Jason pushed to keep his identity from him, but communicated to his mother he was able to understand he'd made the decision as a flawed father who thought it best to protect his son. As far as Xavier, Jace wasn't ready. It nearly broke Xavier when she told him.

She feared how ugly things would get when her past caught up with her. She selfishly wished it would have happened before Xavier made love to her the way he did. He called her the sweetest names and used a voice to speak to her that had her weak in the knees. Destiny had half a mind to show up at Constance Grant's door to ask if she was happy. His mother was to blame for their original separation.

She took back the thought as quickly as it came. If she and Xavier hadn't broken up, she wouldn't have Summer and Junior, and Xavier wouldn't have Zay J. Why did her life have to be so fucking complicated?

Tiffany Best Sister Ever: My flight is delayed, but I should touch down at two

Destiny: I can't wait

Destiny was at an all-time low. Maybe she should see a shrink. But even that could backfire with the size of Tinsville. It was illegal for a professional to discuss her business outside of her sessions, yet her fear of a receptionist reading her inner thoughts and the shameful details of her life caused her to neglect the idea altogether. She hadn't been to church in years.

Destiny recalled how at peace she was when she went. She tried to go back after her parents passed away but couldn't get past how little help they'd been in her time of need. She was an adult now, and a few insincere churchgoers wouldn't keep her from the healing she desperately needed.

She showered and packed her small bag, excited to see her big sister. Tiffany was skilled at the delivery of tough love. She held Destiny accountable in a way that was never shaming. Destiny had little time left to wallow, because Tiffany Davis would remind her that her self-pity was selfish. Tiff would also give her an earful when she found out her baby sister slept with a married man.

Destiny opted to check out of Suite Seduction online. She couldn't face the chipper receptionist who was thrilled about her dirty plans for her stay. There was no way Destiny could tell her the love of her life walked out on her because it was what she deserved.

Just as she was about to start her car, a text from Jason came through.

Jason: We're on the way home now. We should be there in fifteen minutes.

Jason wanted to ensure she have company in their home. *Ugh! I wish.* Before she could send her response, he sent another text.

Jason: Destiny, you there?

She chuckled to herself. Jason had been aloof when it came to her and communication about their kids for years. He was always a good father, but when it came to her, he wasn't interested. Now things had shifted. She had to laugh that it took a pending divorce for them to finally get it right. She was also to blame for how far things had gone. Destiny could have left Jason years ago.

If she was honest, not only had she deserved his treatment, but it simultaneously made her feel superior to him in a way.

Destiny: I don't have company at the house if that's what you're asking. I should be back the same time as you

Jason: Oh, Okay

She arrived at her house moments before Jason and the kids.

"Hey, Mom. What time does Auntie Tiffany get here?" Jace asked when he folded out of the car. He had almost outgrown both their vehicles. Destiny wanted to get him his own car when he turned sixteen, but Jace didn't want to learn to drive. He insisted he could use car ride service anywhere he lived. She and Jason decided it wouldn't be a wise investment to get him a car he refused to drive.

Destiny looked at her phone and saw it was noon. It was a huge relief that he hadn't ignored her like he did most of the week. It would take time to mend their relationship, but for now, she would settle for casual conversation.

"Tiff will be here around two."

"Can I ride with you to the airport?" Summer asked.

Destiny's heart was full. Although she didn't deserve it, she had the most resilient kids. Summer seemed to be open to the changes in her parents' marriage and living arrangements.

"Me too," Junior piped up.

"I don't see why not." Destiny pulled the three of them into a bumbling hug. If she could freeze time for a few hours, she'd keep them in her arms and memorize the moment for the rest of her life.

"Mom," Jace said with his cheek pressed into her shoulder.

"Yeah, Jace."

"Junior stinks."

Summer snatched away and pushed her little brother. "Did you shower?"

They filed into the house as they voiced their concern with Junior's hygiene. Jason leaned against the car and looked in the direction of Xavier's house.

"He wants to take Jace from me."

Destiny chose her words carefully. Jason was a man with feelings, whether they made sense to her or not. Jace was legally an adult. No one could take him from anyone. Destiny exhaled and walked around to the back of the car where Jason was.

"He's eighteen."

Jason peered down at the rocks in their driveway. "You know what I mean."

"I don't. Jace doesn't want to meet him."

Jason's head flew in Destiny's direction. "Who told you that?"

"He did." She twirled a loose piece of her natural hair around her finger.

"Oh."

They sat and watched a neighbor leave the house next to Xavier's. They didn't hide their curious stare at Jason and Destiny.

"I wish I felt bad."

Destiny elbowed Jason in the gut when he smirked.

"He's afraid that he might like Xavier if he meets him. And then maybe he'll hurt you."

"He said that?"

"He didn't have to." Destiny leaned up from the car and stood in front of Jason. "This is going to be a difficult adjustment for everyone.

I don't think any of us will come out unscathed. But no matter how painful this is for us, there's one person who's hurting more."

Jason looked up at her with one eyebrow lifted to the heavens.

"Jace Cooper."

Shock covered Jason's features.

"He'll always be your son. He knows it, but I told him anyway. I wonder what would happen if you told him nothing will change between you whether he decides to develop a relationship with his birth father or not."

Destiny leaned in and hugged Jason's limp body. He wouldn't return the embrace, partly because it was unlike her to initiate physical contact with him. She was sure he was apprehensive to encourage Jace to meet his real dad. But Jace needed his permission, nonetheless.

* * *

Xavier pounded his fist against the countertop. He'd been glued to the front window at his home in hopes that Simone would somehow arrive quicker. He got the shock of his life when he saw Destiny in an embrace with Coop. What the hell would make her hug him?

He couldn't focus on a single train of thought to save his life. Destiny was the last person he wanted to obsess over. Xavier had two children who deserved his attention. He was partly to blame for his time without Zay J. The reality that he would get less time with him settled on Xavier's shoulders as he awaited their return. He hadn't expected to miss them, because he started the night out for drinks with his mentor Donald.

He ended the night home alone with nothing but time and deafening silence. He'd never spent more than three nights away from Zay J. Would that change? What would happen when Simone moved? Would he only see his son during the summer?

Xavier wasn't a heavy drinker, but he found himself with another glass of the dark liquid which seemed to be the only available thing to calm his nerves. He should have been knee-deep in Destiny's pussy before they checked out of Suite Seduction—the pussy she claimed belonged to him. But the sight of her with her arms wrapped around Coop made him want to explode. Xavier was pretty sure he didn't want her, so was it irrational to expect her not to seek comfort somewhere. Coop was her husband.

Fuck! He did want her. He was just so pissed. She'd done the unforgivable when she kept Jace from him. Although he was determined to stuff it down, his true feelings wouldn't allow him the privilege. Even now when he tried to picture the two of them together, the only images his mind presented were of a young, pregnant, or new mom version of Destiny. He'd never seen her in any of those stages, but his mind taunted him with them anyway.

He paced the house like a crazy man. Simone had already communicated that she wanted to spend most of the weekend with Zay J. She said she would be back no later than Sunday morning so both Xavier and their son could prepare for the school and work week. It was only Saturday afternoon. Time suddenly moved slowly. How the hell was he supposed to fill it now that he couldn't stomach Destiny?

Xavier changed into his workout gear and headed for the next best thing. The community center was as new as the Tinsville High School. It was a good thing for the town as far as crime. When the youth had somewhere to go, there was a direct correlation in a reduction of crime. But as a money guy, Xavier could only imagine how much they put up for the facility in comparison to their current profit.

He couldn't wait to start work on Monday. Once he got involved with the schools' issues, his brain wouldn't busy itself with problems he couldn't solve. Xavier quickly purchased a membership. The teen must have been confused when he hesitated over the family membership question. It was a simple question that gave him major pause. He eventually decided to include two additional members to his account.

He and Simone were still married on paper. Then there was the possibility that maybe he and his sons could visit the center every week until Jace left for school or when he was home for break. *Wishful thinking*. The squeaky sound of sneakers filled the air. Xavier instantly relaxed.

He grabbed a ball and shot around for almost an hour without breaking a real sweat. He needed to be pushed, and he couldn't do that alone.

"We need another person. You wanna run one?"

Xavier saw five teenagers who reminded him of his former Tinsville Jaguars basketball team. He smirked to himself at the memory and how he was certain he was a man at that age. Now, these boys looked like babies.

"This old man can't run," one of the smaller boys said under his breath. He turned his back and waved his hand dismissively.

Xavier threw his ball at the kid's ankle, which caused him to trip. His friends roared with laughter. Xavier saw the kid when he came into the gym and was impressed with his ball handling skills. He also found the kid to be arrogant and looked forward to knocking him off his pedestal.

"I got time today."

The three-on-three game ended with Xavier and his team ahead. They won ten to the snarky kid's team at seven. Xavier hobbled to the side to grab water when he heard a familiar voice.

"You getting old, Grant."

He was too tired to hurl a comeback. Instead, he shook his head at Coach Donald Archer in hopes he'd leave him be.

"Imagine my surprise when I'm doing my laps and I see my former Jaguar in a three-on-three game with the current Jaguars."

Xavier wasn't surprised they were on the team. They had skills.

"You gave them a run for their money. They just won state two months ago."

Xavier's eyebrows flew up. No wonder his body ached all over. He felt his phone vibrate and hoped it was Zay J. It was a call from Destiny. What could she possibly want with him? Unless she wanted to give him his son's number, he didn't have the energy to speak to her right now. He sent the call to voicemail.

Archer's observant eyes regarded his mentee. "What the hell happened to you last night."

Xavier stood from the floor and took a seat near his mentor on the gray bleachers. The hoop nearest them was occupied by a dad and an eight- or nine-year-old kid. The sight pulled at his heartstrings. Not only had he never had the privilege of that kind of intimacy with his father, he would never experience Jace at that age.

"I couldn't do it."

Archer shifted his body toward Xavier.

"That's from all that shit people eat today. And all that time on them damn devices. You ain't got no testosterone."

"What?"

"I'm saying, shit like this ain't supposed to happen until you much older than me. I do just fine, by the way." Archer tugged on his jacket and puffed his chest with pride.

"Wait. You think I couldn't perform?"

"You said you couldn't do it."

Xavier choked on his spit. "Damn, that's cold. My body wanted to do it. Shit, we'd already done it earlier this week."

Coach Archer stood and slapped Xavier on the back of his head.

"Damn, Coach. What was that for?"

He sat back down with a satisfied grin on his face. "One, watch your damn mouth. And two, you're married, and you slept with a married woman."

"I told you it was complicated."

"Was this before or after you found out about the kid?"

Xavier still had his hand at his nape where his mentor slapped him. Archer had old man strength. "After."

He shook his head. "Well, what the hell happened last night, since you say you don't have a problem performing?" Archer used his fingers to make air quotes.

"She booked us a hotel, and when I got there, she had her cheeks out and her titties pushed up." The older man glared at him, so he decided to adjust his language. "She was dressed scantily clad."

"Grant, you's a damn fool, you know that? I'm still not hearing an issue."

"The problem was I kept seeing her pregnant and holding our baby in her arms. I didn't know her when she looked like that. It was strange how real the visions were. Felt like I was losing my mind."

Xavier held his breath for what his coach would say. He hadn't intended to tell anyone what happened the night before. He figured he'd use basketball and work to occupy his mind, and maybe it would go away on its own.

"Is that crazy?" If he wasn't out of his mind, his coach's silence would push him over the edge.

"Sounds like your heart won't let you rush what your mind swears you want."

Archer saw the confused look on Xavier's face.

"When's the last time you been to church?"

Xavier blew out a breath. Why couldn't he give him advice that made sense.

"It's been a while," Xavier admitted.

"You're in luck. My wife and I are attending First Baptist tomorrow morning."

"I don't know, Coach."

Archer stood and moved his hand like he'd slap Xavier again, but Xavier guarded his head this time.

"Suit yourself. If you change your mind, call me. I'm not responding to no damn texts."

Chapter Nine

"Dee!"

"Tiff!"

The sisters embraced each other like they'd never let go. People walked around them to get to their designated cars, but it didn't dull their moment.

"I'm so glad you're here."

"Ow," Tiffany said when Destiny pinched her.

"I just wanted to make sure you're real."

"Where are my babies?" Tiffany asked once they had her luggage secure in the trunk.

"I told Jason I wanted to have time to chat with you. Summer and Junior were pissed, but Jason bribed them with ice cream."

Destiny chuckled, but her smile didn't reach her eyes. She prayed her sister would give her time before she called her out on it.

"You look good, sissy. I know you're going through a rough patch, but you're glowing."

Destiny's cheeks flushed.

Tiffany shifted her body in the passenger side. *Shit. Here we go!*

"You fucked Zay?"

Destiny stole a glance at her sister, whose face was void of emotion. She'd rather Tiffany be pissed. Destiny couldn't handle any more disappointment from someone she loved.

"He fucked me."

A thick silence filled the vehicle.

Finally, Tiffany howled with laughter. "You're crazy. Y'all used to go at it like cats and dogs back in the day. I couldn't stand y'all asses."

Destiny smiled because she'd snuck Xavier into their house plenty of times after their parents went to sleep. They never heard a peep, but Tiffany and Destiny shared a wall.

"What about his wife?"

"She's with Jeff."

"Who the hell is Jeff?"

"I don't know. Something about him only marrying her because she got pregnant." Destiny's eyes misted. She made a mess of her life, and she genuinely couldn't picture a worse outcome. At least her kids had come around. She was grateful for that.

Tiffany reached over and grasped her sister's free hand. "I'm sorry, Dee."

Destiny drove them forty minutes from the airport to Tinsville and filled her in on all the latest details with her and Jason.

"We decided to use a mediator for everything instead of going to court."

"You sound much calmer than I thought you would. You're talking divorce, Dee."

"I know."

"No, you don't. I love you, Destiny."

"Why do I feel like there's a big hairy butt coming?"

"Because there is. There's a reason weddings happen in church and divorces in the court."

Destiny wanted to stay in La La Land where, somehow, she and Xavier skipped off into the sunset. But once again, her big sister was right. She needed to focus on Jace, Summer, and Junior. Then she could address her love life after her divorce was final.

"I thought you would be happy. You've never liked Jason."

"I can't stand his ass. But you've been with him for eighteen years. You still have to coparent with him. What is he going to do for work?"

Destiny genuinely hadn't considered it. Would he expect her to pay her bills and his? She'd been too preoccupied with Xavier's anger to get her house in order. She'd thanked God her sister was here to talk some sense into her and support her while she figured things out. From here on out, Destiny's energy would be directed toward what mattered most—on her children and how the hell she and Jason would raise them.

They pulled into the driveway and found the kids seated on the porch. They piled out of the car, and Tiffany accosted them with clumsy hugs.

"Oh my gosh, Jace. You're so big and handsome. When did this happen?" Tiffany pulled on the facial hair that hung from his chin. "I have not been away that long."

"He had a growth shirt," Junior said.

"Growth spurt, man," Jace corrected.

"Look at my babies." Tiffany pulled Junior and Summer into another tight hug.

"Hi, Auntie Tiffany!" Summer squealed.

"How old are you?" she asked while she pushed her hair aside to see her face better.

"Fourteen."

Tiffany's eyes bulged. Destiny shrugged. Her babies were all beautiful, but Summer had become a stunning young woman. She was undeniable. Tiffany would take her niece on their shopping ritual that would inevitably end in a tense conversation between her and Jason about appropriate clothes for a teenager.

"Girl, you look like your mom at that age." Tiffany's face contorted in confusion. "What is this?"

There was urgency in her sister's voice and fear in her daughter's eyes. Upon close inspection, there was a bruise on Summer's arm.

"Who did this to you?" Destiny asked loud enough for Jason to hear. He made his way outside and nodded at Tiff when he did.

"It's not that big of a deal, Mom."

"Yes, the hell it is. Who hit you?"

"Jace, why don't you and Junior help me with my bags, and show me where I'm going to be sleeping," Tiffany said to the boys.

"But I wanna hear who hit Summer," Junior insisted.

Tiffany and Jace shared a quiet laugh and explained to him why it was best Summer have privacy.

"You'll find out what happened eventually," Jace said as they stepped into the house.

Destiny was grateful for Tiff's intervention. She didn't want to embarrass Summer if she'd lost her first fight. Or God forbid, if a boy put his hands on her.

"Please tell us what happened."

Summer rolled her eyes and crossed her arms. She had her phone tucked in her hand which would serve as a major distraction. Destiny swiped it.

"You can have this back as soon as we're done. Are you in some kind of trouble?"

"No, ma'am. You should see what I did to her face."

"Thank God," Jason said. Relief covered his face, and he gave her a high-five.

"Jason."

"Your mom's right. You still need to tell us what happened."

Summer's eyes swung across the street and stayed there. "Summer. Answer me."

"Santana said Jace wasn't my real brother."

Destiny couldn't hold back her gasp. "She said what?"

"She said Jace looks more like this other boy in our school... Xavier Grant, Jr."

Jason cursed under his breath and put his hands on his head.

"Everybody agreed, and said they were twins." Summer's light brown skin reddened as she recounted what happened.

"When was this?" Destiny asked. It was unnerving how accurate the children had been.

"Friday. I almost got suspended, but the cafeteria lady backed up my story. I tried to walk away like you always tell me, Mama. But she started calling Jace a Daddy's Maybe."

"A what?" Jason's fists were clenched.

"I guess it means they think Jace isn't yours... like Mom would do something like that. You're the one who cheated."

"That's enough!" Destiny yelled. If she didn't set her straight, Jason would lose Summer forever. "Inside, right now. We'll talk about your punishment for fighting and not telling us about it later."

Jason stood planted in his place. He didn't want to have this conversation with their fourteen and ten-year-old children. It was hard enough to explain it to Jace, but it needed to happen. Summer's classmates had unknowingly forced their hand.

Tiffany had a video game console in her hand and moved it dramatically in the air. Jace and Junior taunted her about it, but she was determined not to get left behind. When she saw Summer and Destiny, she put it on pause.

"What's wrong?"

"Sit down," Destiny commanded. She didn't bother to respond to her sister. Tiffany could stay or leave, but she needed to lay her cards on the table. It was truth time.

"Kids, there's something I need to tell you."

"You already said you and Daddy are breaking up. We know," Junior said, annoyed.

"Yes, baby. We're breaking up, but there's more."

"Shit," Jace said under his breath.

"Hey," Tiffany said and hit him with a pillow. "I don't care if you eighteen or fifty. Don't curse around me."

"Yes, ma'am."

"Jace is your brother. He'll always be your brother. And Jason is your father. But before I met Daddy, I was already pregnant with Jace."

"What? So it's true? Santana was right?" Summer bolted from her seat.

Jason walked over to where she stood in tears and pulled her into his arms. "I knew."

She reared her head back in disbelief. "You did?"

"I'm confused," Junior announced. "If Dad ain't Jace's dad, who is?"

"Xavier Grant," Destiny revealed.

Junior stood. "How can a boy at Summer's school be Jace's dad? I'm little, but I know that ain't right."

"The boy at Summer's school is not my dad. He's my brother," Jace told him.

Junior slapped his hands on his cheeks in shock. It was hard to be in a somber mood with this kid around. They all chuckled to themselves at his inability to process such a big moment.

"But I'm your brother."

"That's right. Xavier Grant is my birth father. And he was a son who is a junior like you. I have two brothers."

"Why are you so cool about this?" Summer asked from Jason's shoulder.

"I wasn't. That's why I moved out."

"Moved out?" Tiffany asked, then slapped her hand across her mouth. "Sorry. I don't mean to interrupt."

"It's OK, Auntie Tiffany. Mom and I talked, and I realized she was my age when she got pregnant. She thought my birth dad wouldn't want me. Then our father had the bright idea to hide it from us so we wouldn't get hurt," Jace said with a significant amount of sarcasm in his voice.

"Is he nice?" Junior asked.

Jace looked from Destiny to Jason. "I don't want to meet him."

"Why?" Junior kept on. "If I had two dads," Junior jumped up and whirled around the room, "I would never have any bullies."

They laughed again at his innocence. He was the breath of fresh air everyone didn't know they needed.

"Does anyone have any other questions?"

"Is this the real reason you're breaking up?" Summer asked.

Destiny hated how much this situation forced her to grow up. It was bound to happen eventually. She just didn't think it would be like this.

"It's one of the many reasons. But your father and I weren't nice to each other long before Xavier moved back in town."

"I have a question," Jace said.

Destiny's heart rate increased. The younger ones, she could handle, but Jace moved like an adult these days. His questions weren't easy.

"Of course. What is it?"

"Did he know? Because when I saw him in the driveway, I knew immediately. I had a lot of time to think this week, and if he did know, I would imagine he would try to hug me."

Destiny dropped her head.

"So, you kept it from me *and* him?" There was judgment in his voice, judgment she deserved.

She nodded, because the words wouldn't come. Destiny prayed. At that moment, she asked for forgiveness for her actions. She prayed Jace would eventually have a relationship with both of his dads. She prayed for Jason and his mental health through their situation. She sent healing energy toward Xavier through his separation and toward the pain he held for all the time he missed with Jace. And she prayed that Summer and Junior would maintain a shred of their innocence and trust in others.

Small arms wrapped around her. It was Summer. "I'm sorry you're hurting, Mama. Jace said you were his age when you got pregnant."

"I was. But that's not an excuse. I should have told him and Xavier a long time ago."

"We all make mistakes, remember?"

Destiny hugged Summer tightly. Her family knew the truth.

They may have had more questions, but they'd covered the most important details. Now the healing could begin.

* * *

Xavier insisted that Zay J attend service with him on Sunday morning. He wasn't thrilled about it, but when he learned there was a basketball gym attached where he could play during youth service, he quickly got onboard. Simone thanked Xavier for the invite but respectfully declined. She said she would rather spend time alone while Xavier Jr. was with his father. A call from Destiny came through just as Xavier was about to tell Zay J it was time to go.

"Yeah?"

He could hear Destiny steady her breath. He was abrupt with her, because now wasn't the time. Xavier couldn't get past the images that continued to populate in his mind's eye when he thought about her. His coach was right. It had been a week since his life was turned upside down and he learned he had an adult son.

The fact that he still cared deeply for Destiny made things worse. She wasn't some random woman from his past. She was the woman from his dreams. She held a space in his heart and soul that no other woman occupied. And she'd carried his firstborn son... without him.

"I wanted to give you a heads up that my daughter got into a fight at school about Xavier Jr."

"What? What happened?"

"The kids taunted her because Jace and Xavier Jr. look so much alike. She got into a physical altercation when they called Jace a Daddy's Maybe."

"The hell?"

"I told Summer and Junior about you. I didn't want you to be caught off guard if Xavier Jr. has questions. I imagine he'll be approached if he hasn't already."

"Damn. Thank you for calling, Destiny."

"Of course. Bye, Xavier."

The line disconnected, and he felt a sudden emptiness. He was still mad, but he also loved her. Why couldn't time fast forward? He was sure he'd be in a better space eventually. What if she couldn't wait for him? What if she accepted that their relationship didn't stand a chance, and she learned to live on her own?

Xavier couldn't stress over that now. Destiny's children knew Jace was his. That meant they knew Jace had a brother who lived across the street. After church, he would explain everything to Zay J the best he could.

"Let's go, son."

First Baptist Church was a breath of fresh air. Everywhere Xavier looked, he was met with a welcomed and loving face. Several of the women seemed interested, even though he still wore his ring. He hadn't bothered to take it off. On the rare occasion he did take it off to shower or lotion, he put it back on because it was a habit.

Xavier wasn't the only one who garnered extra attention. He noted that a group of girls giggled and whispered among themselves when they saw his son. The smile on Zay J's face let Xavier know he wouldn't have any issues getting him back to church. The service started with upbeat music. Although Xavier's life was unstable, his coach had been spot on about his need to attend service.

Xavier hadn't belonged to a church since he left his hometown. It was the reason he was a man of integrity to this day. The right thing to do was to marry Simone when she got pregnant. It was what was best for Zay J. Now he wasn't so sure. It was wrong to sleep with Destiny while they were both married, but it certainly didn't feel wrong.

He still believed in God; he just hadn't made it around to finding a church home since Tinsville. In the city he moved to, the pastors were more concerned with bigger buildings and more offerings. The prosperity message didn't sit well with Xavier. He was skilled on the ways to make money, but he couldn't respect men who earned their wealth from poor people. How could they have the finest facilities with members who couldn't feed their family?

The small town of Tinsville took care of their own. If a member was in need, they were sure to look out for their own. Had anyone helped Destiny when her parents were killed? Did they help her with Jace? The last song was led by a girl who couldn't have been much older than Zay J. The powerful timber of her voice paired with the meaning of the words that urged the congregation to hold out until morning made Xavier's eyes mist.

She sang about the need for believers to keep the faith through the night. Then everything would be alright. The confusion in his mind lifted. He still didn't know how things would turn out, but he was sure his family would be fine. The choir took their seats, and the announcements started.

He remembered how bored he'd been as a child when he attended church with his mother years ago. Now that he was older, he was familiar with the people on the sick and shut in list. He sent up prayers for each of them. The children and young adults were released to their own service. Zay J stood.

"Aye, man. I hate to say this, but it's creepy people everywhere. You got your phone?"

"Yeah, old man." Zay J laughed at Xavier and followed behind the group of girls they saw at the start of service. He shook his head and returned his focus to the pulpit.

The pastor took the pulpit and prayed for the congregation. He opened his bible and shared the title of his sermon— "When God is trying to tell you something."

Xavier hung onto every word the pastor said, and after the service, he was relieved of the heaviness he'd carried. He met several people from the community. Most of them he recognized, and a few were new faces. One of the gentlemen was a coworker from the Tinsville City Schools. He expressed their excitement about Xavier's first day on Monday.

Xavier was able to say hello to Coach Archer and his wife. Archer agreed to show him where the infamous basketball court was where the kids hung out during and after church.

"I'm proud of you, Grant."

"What chu mean?"

"You showed up. That's half the battle."

Xavier nodded.

"Look, I know it can't be easy to focus on what's ahead of you with this new position when your home life is... complicated."

"That's one way to look at it."

"But you are. And I'm proud of you," Archer said.

"Don't start crying," Xavier teased.

"You better be glad we're in the house of the Lord and I can't cuss you out."

They made their way into the pristine gym, and Xavier immediately spotted his son. He was much taller than the other kids his age.

"Zay J, come here. I want you to meet someone."

Xavier introduced Archer to his son, and they shot the ball for about twenty more minutes before they headed out. On the car ride home, Xavier decided to address the new elephant in the room.

"I need to talk to you about something."

"What happened?" Zay J asked with wide eyes.

"Before Mom, I dated someone else," Xavier started.

"Is that all? I know you weren't a virgin before Mom, if that's what you're getting at."

Xavier howled with laughter. "No more reality television for you."

Zay J laughed too.

"I'm serious though. I had a high school sweetheart here in Tinsville."

"A high school what?"

"It's like a super serious girlfriend."

"Oh."

"She got pregnant before I moved away to college, but I just found out this week."

"Is this why you and mom are breaking up?" Zay J had his face in his phone, but Xavier learned it was more of a habit than evidence he wasn't tuned in to the conversation.

"Kind of. I don't know how to explain it. The kid was mine."

"What does that mean?"

"It means you have a brother."

Zay J's head shot up and flew in his dad's direction. He pulled into the driveway and shifted his body toward his son. A small smile spread across his face.

"What? You're not mad?"

"No. I'm not your wife."

Xavier pushed his face playfully. "It's OK if you are."

"When can I meet him?"

"You serious?"

"Yeah, Dad. I'm an only child, and you're telling me I have a brother."

"Yep."

"When can I meet him?"

Xavier paused. When would he meet his brother? When would Xavier meet his son?

"It's kind of a good news, bad news with this situation."

"What?"

"It's the tall kid across the street."

Zay J's head craned to peek behind them in the direction of Destiny's house. "Summer Cooper's older brother."

"Yeah, why?"

"Some of the kids said we look alike. I haven't seen him up close or anything, so I didn't understand why she got upset. Makes sense now."

Xavier grasped his shoulder. It was a lot for anyone to take in.

"When can I meet him?"

It was as though Zay J's resiliency meter was off the charts. It brought a smile to Xavier's heart.

"Right now, he doesn't want to meet me. So, I don't know, son. I honestly don't know."

Chapter Ten

It was time to take Tiffany back to the airport. She'd kept her word and stayed as long as Destiny needed. It had been a month of painful yet necessary moments. Jason shut her out when he started openly dating someone new. It wasn't that there was another woman in the picture, it was his unwillingness to allow her to have a say on how they approached the subject with the kids.

Destiny leaned on Tiffany until it was unfair to keep her around. She'd gotten over the sting that Xavier hadn't spoken to her since she called him to tell him her other children knew. She and Jace communicated often, and he'd even divulged his fear about his big move in a few weeks. They were in a routine. The kids were with her Monday through Thursday, and they were with Jason from Friday through Sunday.

Destiny and Jason had their first mediation concerning the divorce last week, and she was relieved to get the process started. He filed the separation paperwork, because one of his women told him it would expedite the divorce. So far, they had mostly signed papers.

The biggest change since Tiff arrived was that Jason got a job.

His confidence was through the roof, and for the sake of her children, Destiny was happy for him.

"I still miss him," Destiny said as she walked through the doors of the airport with Tiffany. She paid for parking because she wasn't ready for their time to be done.

"I know."

"What do I do?"

Tiffany sighed. "I gotta be honest. When I first got here, the last thing I wanted to hear about was your feelings for Xavier. But seeing you put your home back in order the way you have, I say go for it."

Destiny's lip trembled. "What?"

"But—"

"I should've known there was a but."

"You've got to figure out him and Jace first. I understand you don't want to push Jace. But at some point, it's not up to him to make the first move. You're the adult. Bring them together, and whatever they do after that isn't up to you. Everything else will fall into place. I promise you."

Destiny pulled her big sister in for another tight hug. She let the tears roll down her cheeks as Tiffany squeezed her tighter.

"I love you, sis. I'm so glad you came. I needed this."

Tiffany stepped back. "Mama woulda been proud of you."

Destiny tried to wipe her eyes, but every time she did, they filled again.

"Daddy woulda called you a cry baby," she added.

Destiny shrugged. "He sure would have. Call me when you land."

"OK. Tell my babies I love them."

"I will."

Destiny's mind reeled as she considered her sister's words on the drive back to Tinsville. She had her sister's blessing to go for it with Xavier. She giggled to herself. Tiffany's approval was still so important to her.

Destiny saw Xavier ride bikes with Zay J in their neighborhood over the past few weeks. She saw him in the morning on his way to work. He was breathtaking in his business casual. What surprised her the most was how much peace radiated from him.

She waved to him when it was obvious they'd seen each other, and he returned her waves with polite nods. As Destiny made her way home, it dawned on her how she'd bring Jace and Xavier together. And if her gossiping co-workers were right, she could do it this afternoon. Last week, Destiny overheard two of her younger *Upundies* employees gush over a beautiful man who worked out religiously at the youth center. When they described his hazel eyes, she knew it was Xavier.

Destiny: Can you meet me at home?

Jace and Destiny were close again. She had put in the work to rebuild their relationship by being truthful with him. She was confident she'd regained his trust, but he hadn't moved back in. He told her it was his version of a trial run for his official move out of town for school. Destiny supported his decision. The family needed the slow transition as much as he did. In the past weeks, she'd gotten somewhat accustomed to only Summer and Junior in the house. And she'd finally accepted things as they were.

Jace: Of course. Everything okay?

Destiny: Yes.

Jason's father lived less than five minutes away. By the time Destiny showered and redressed, Jace sat in the living room engulfed in an anime cartoon.

"Hey, Ma." Jace stood and leaned down to give Destiny a hug.

"Hey, son. You ready?"

"Maybe."

Destiny grabbed her keys and asked, "You trust me?"

Jace stood in full contemplation. He wouldn't respond until he was ready.

"I do."

"Remember that when we get there."

Destiny and Jace piled into her car. She let him select the music and prayed the entire ride. *Let Xavier be there. Please let Jace be open to speak to him. Forgive me for waiting this long to bring his son to him. Forgive me for keeping this man from his child.*

"You brought me to the youth center? Is this about volunteering? I already got into college, Mom."

Destiny pushed him in the arm. "Get out."

They walked side by side to the entrance of the gymnasium. "And we don't just volunteer to list it on an application or resume."

Destiny paid for a day pass while the rhythm of her heart tripled. The girls at her work mentioned they spotted Xavier in the gym in the late afternoon.

"You good, Mom?"

Destiny peered up at Jace. "You trust me?" she asked again.

"Yes."

They walked down the stairs because the entry was at the top level, while the court was located beneath it. The sounds of men's grunts and the smell of musty bodies sent Destiny's senses into overload. There was no way she could turn back now. Several hoops were occupied with small crowds and players engulfed in pick-up games.

Xavier shot the ball alone at one of the basketball courts opposite the entryway.

"You gotta be kiddin' me," Jace blurted.

Destiny shifted her body to face her son but allowed her gaze to bounce between them. "It's not your job to fix this or come to me and say you want to meet him. After today, it's up to you how much contact you have with him."

Jace's shoulders slouched, and he had the same look on his face he got when she made him do chores. Xavier noticed them and stood motionless. Destiny saw fear in his eyes. It was a gamble to bring them together without their consent, but this was the best way. Jace wouldn't run away like he did weeks ago in the driveway, because now he had all the facts.

Destiny gave him one last glance, then headed toward Xavier, confident their son would follow.

"Xavier. This is Jace. Jace, baby, this is Xavier Grant."

The two of them stood and regarded each other silently. She saw the tear escape Xavier's eye. He used his shirt to wipe it along with the sweat on his brow. Destiny berated herself for the direction her thoughts took when she saw that marvelous happy trail—fully aware of where it ended.

"You wanna play?" Xavier asked.

Jace nodded.

Destiny stepped aside as they fell into an easy game of one on one. In no time, Jace relaxed, and the two of them wore matching smiles.

"Jace."

They both turned their heads and gave her their full attention. It was eerie how many gestures they had in common.

"I'll be upstairs. Call me when you're done."

"I can bring him home," Xavier offered. "I mean, if you're okay with it," he said to Jace.

"That would be cool. Is that alright with you, Mom?"

Praise God! She held back her tears. This was their moment. "Yes, son. That's alright with me."

* * *

Xavier was on cloud nine at work. He loved Mondays, but today took the cake, although he was impossibly sore. His body ached because he spent over an hour in a one-on-one game with his son the night before. Jace was a cool kid. He was respectful, level headed, and good looking. He'd take full credit for the latter, but Destiny and Coop did a hell of a job on the former.

On the ride home, they talked about the college Jace would attend in September which was a month away. It bothered him how little time there was before his son would move, but Xavier thanked God Jace was open to know him at all. He didn't have those visions when he saw Destiny. Maybe because a fully grown Jace was with her or because she'd put herself aside and did what was best for him and their child this time.

He noticed how fine she was without immediately getting angry with her. Jace told him about the major he selected and surprised him when he asked Xavier what he went to school for. He was impressed with what Xavier did for work and said it would be a blessing if Xavier could bring more money into Tinsville.

Xavier's chest tightened when he observed how mature his son was. When Xavier pulled up to Destiny's house, Jace thanked him for the game and the ride. He asked if they could exchange numbers. He also asked if he could meet his brother. Xavier's voice broke when he told him Xavier Jr. had asked to meet him many times already.

"You must have had some kind of night, Grant, or you figured out the answer to our deficit," Richard joked and interrupted Xavier's thoughts. Richard Robinson was an older guy who worked in finance. He was a smart man with very little applicable knowledge. Richard wanted well for the town of Tinsville, but he was also threatened by Xavier's risky approach.

Xavier's suggestion would turn Richard's world upside down. They could play it safe and remain in debt, or they could take some calculated risks and not only come out of the red, but they could also finally reside in the green.

"Yes, to both. I had an amazing night, and I have an idea how to get us out of our money problem."

Richard's eyes ballooned.

"Can you set up a meeting with Travis and the rest of the team?" Travis was the CEO. Xavier could request a meeting, but it would happen much faster if Richard did.

"You're serious?"

"As a heart attack."

"I'll do it. But we don't joke about heart attacks around here," Richard said and gave Xavier a side eye.

Before Xavier could apologize, he got a text from Jace.

Jace: Hey. Are you still mad at my mom?

Shit! Destiny wouldn't be crazy enough to ask Jace to text me, would she?

Xavier: *Why you ask that?*

Jace: *She likes you*

Xavier: *I like her too*

Jace: *oh. Well she seems sad and I wondered if you were as mad as I was*

Xavier: *I am. But not as much now that I got to meet you*

Jace: *she'd kill me if she knew I said this, but you need to thank her. I would have never asked to meet you. She didn't tell me I was coming to meet you yesterday*

Xavier: *I didn't know either*

Jace: *I could tell. You was cryin' *crying laughing emoji

Xavier: *you got jokes. You remember who won yesterday*

Jace: *yeah you won by two points, but I bet you're icing your knees and back to*

Xavier: *how many ways can you call me old*

Jace: *I gotta go. Can I call you later?*

Xavier's heart swelled. He found out he had an adult son. Once he knew, he wanted to move heaven and earth to be with him, but Jace didn't want to. Xavier wouldn't force himself on Jace, but he prayed they'd have some kind of relationship before Jace left for college. His prayers had been answered.

Xavier: *I'd love that*

Jace: *you ain't over there cryin' are you?*

Xavier swiped a single tear from his face and chuckled to himself. *This kid is funny.*

Xavier: *Sweating laughing emoji

Xavier stood from his chair and decided he would get out of his office and take a walk. It was a beautiful summer day, and until the team agreed to meet with him and approved his plan, there wasn't much work for him to do. Destiny was heavy on his mind. In the past month, he and Simone started the divorce process. It was tough on Zay J, but they did their best to remain as present in his life as they did when they all lived together.

He pulled out his cell phone and called her.

"Xavier?"

"Yeah, it's me."

"Is everything okay with Jace?"

"Yeah. He's... great. You and Coop did a good job with him."

She released a breath. "Thank you."

"You're welcome."

He held the phone and listened to her breathe. They did that a lot when they were younger.

"Are you okay, Zay? Are you still upset with me?"

"I'm good, better now that I've met Jace. He texted me a bit ago."

Destiny giggled. "That's good. If Jace takes time to text you or respond to your texts, he likes you."

"He's called me old in every language."

Destiny laughed loud and from her gut. The sound brought a smile to his face. "He does that."

"He said you seem sad."

"He what?"

"You can't tell him you know. He'll never tell me anything again." Xavier stepped on the path around a lake several yards from his office.

"What else did he say?"

"He said you like me."

Destiny gasped.

"Do you... like me?"

Her breaths morphed into a moan, and his body hardened.

"I never stopped, Zay."

"Wanna know what I told Jace?"

"Maybe," she said nervously.

"I said I like you too."

Destiny released another one of her breaths like she held it while she awaited his response.

"What do we do now?" Destiny asked.

"You let me take you out."

Destiny was quiet for so long he looked to make sure the line hadn't disconnected.

"What's wrong?"

"Nothing. It's just that I know I've been self-centered."

Xavier nodded. He loved Destiny, but she was right. She had been self-focused in the past. Not in a vain way, but in her inability to see how her choices affected anyone but herself.

"I've had a lot of time to think since Jason moved out and while Tiffany was here. And I don't want to lose focus. My highest priority is your relationship with Jace. I want him to meet your son—"

"They beat you to it. Zay J asked when he could meet Jace, and Jace asked yesterday if he could meet Zay J."

"That's great," Destiny said.

"But?"

"You said you want to take me out. And I want to go. I just... I won't sleep with a married man again. Not while I'm also still technically married."

Xavier listened. He respected her stance, and somehow, it turned him on. He didn't want to say the filthy things in his mind, so he said nothing.

"Jason and I started with a mediator though. We don't have a lot of assets, just what my parents left me and Tiff. And Jason told them he didn't want it. He basically wanted shared custody in writing and stipulations on how far I can move his children. I'm rambling."

"I miss you."

"Did you hear what I said?"

"Yes, baby. I heard you."

"Then no sexy talk."

"Define sexy."

Destiny giggled. "Nothing that will get me all hot and bothered while we're still married."

"When your divorce is final, I can talk freaky to you?"

"When *both* of our divorces are final."

"Dayum."

Destiny laughed. "I don't want any bad juju or energy on me because I kept sleeping with you while you're with Simone."

"I'm not with Simone—"

"I know. She's with Jeff. But legally, she's still your wife. Either of you could change your mind."

"Is that what you're afraid of? Me changing my mind?"

"You could."

"I'm still at work, so I need to go soon. But this is why I want to take you out. I'll keep my hands to myself. I just want you to know, I've worked through some things, and now that I have, I want to be in your space again. I still want you, Dee Dee."

"Yes. You can take me out."

"Hell yeah!" Xavier pumped his fist. He would move as slow as he needed to. He would honor her wishes and keep his hands to himself. Besides, it would make the next time even more special. Now he just had to figure out how fucking long two divorces would take.

* * *

Destiny buzzed around the house with pep in her step. She meant it when she said she wouldn't sleep with Zay again until their divorces were final. She was floored at how well he took her admission. From the inflection in his voice, he took it as a challenge. Not to get her to change her mind, but to do whatever it would take for them to be back together again.

Destiny had so much to be thankful for. Never in a million years did she think there would be a world where she could be with Xavier Grant again. She kept the same energy, days after their conversation, during her short shift at work. One of the girls needed to come late, so Destiny covered the gap of a few hours between them. As she bopped around the store, she hummed and praised God. She decided, at that moment, it was time for her to go back to church to thank Him in person.

"Do you have this in a small?" a masculine voice asked behind her.

Destiny clutched her chest. She hadn't realized she had a customer. She focused her eyes on the attractive man, and her heart leaped. It was the most romantic gesture when men came to the store to buy gifts for the women in their life. The gold color of the lingerie was sexy. She could see why he chose it.

"I do. Can I help you find anything else?"

The man wet his lips and took Destiny in from head to toe. She blushed at the attention. That happened to her more often over the past few weeks. When she was with Jason, men rarely approached her because she was always so stressed. Once Xavier's hands touched her, it was as though her sleeping sensuality rose to the surface. And alluring men like the one in front of her noticed.

He cleared his throat. "This is enough. I'm too afraid to buy perfume. I don't know what she likes."

Destiny's smile widened. "There's nothing more touching than a scent selected by your man. Even if she wouldn't have picked it, she'll wear it because you like it."

"That makes a lot of sense. I see why they have you out front."

Destiny led him to the counter and showed him the perfume display while she grabbed the item in a small. When she returned, he had two bottles of perfume in his hand.

"Here, use these." She picked up two white strips and sprayed each with a different scent.

The man put them under his nose and easily chose the one he liked best. Satisfied with her work, Destiny rounded the corner and rang up his items. "What's the special occasion?"

"It's gonna sound wild."

"Wild doesn't scare me," Destiny flirted. It was innocent in nature. Charm went a long way with male customers. And he was cute. If she would be on her best behavior with Xavier, she needed something to pass the time.

"My girlfriend is getting a divorce."

"Well damn," Destiny responded. It was none of her business the nature of this man's relationship.

He settled the bill and collected the lilac-colored gift bags.

"Thank you for your help today..." he started.

"Destiny. I'm Destiny."

He held his hand out, and she shook it politely.

"Jeff."

Destiny's throat went dry. *He couldn't be. Is this Simone's Jeff?*

Jeff winked at her and threw her one last smile and left a speechless Destiny with her mouth wide open.

She returned home shortly after her shift and paced the floor as she contemplated whether she should call Xavier. It was Thursday, and they hadn't spoken since he called on Monday. Destiny didn't want to seem thirsty, but she was eager to know when he would take her out.

Destiny: hey

Her phone rang in her hand, and she almost dropped it in her glass of juice. She shook her head at her fumble and calmed her mind as she accepted Xavier's call.

"Hey," she answered.

"You said no sexy talk."

"What are you talking about?"

"I'm talking about me trying to concentrate at work and getting a 'heyyyyy baby' text from you." Xavier exaggerated the hey and made his voice sound overly sexual.

"You got all of that from one word?"

"Yep. Why you 'hey' texting me, woman?"

"Ummm."

There was noise in Xavier's background as he moved to a different location.

"Can you hear me?" he asked.

"Yes. How's work going?"

"It's good. I have a big meeting with the CEO and the rest of the team tomorrow. I'm nervous."

"Is this a shake shit up kind of meeting?"

Xavier's throaty laughter sent sensual chills up her spine. "What you know about shaking shit up?"

"I know you. And if they let you in the room, you're going to tell them exactly how to make things better."

"Dayum, girl."

"Are you ready?"

"For the meeting?" Xavier's flirty nature put Destiny at ease. They'd been hot and heavy, no contact, and now this. She had no complaints.

"Yes, Zay, for the meeting."

"There you go with that sexy talk."

Destiny guffawed. "You so crazy."

"I'm ready. I didn't want to over prepare. This is more of an intro to an unorthodox solution to the school's deficit."

A small whimper escaped Destiny's lips. "You said no sexy talk."

Xavier chuckled. "And what was sexy about what I said, Dee Dee?"

"You're using words like deficit and saying you're ready."

"What about fiscal responsibility and spreadsheets?" He taunted her.

Destiny cleared her throat. She grabbed a piece of mail from the countertop and fanned herself. She'd always been attracted to Xavier's mind. He was a breath of fresh air when he spoke, and easy on the eyes too.

"What's your million-dollar idea?" she asked to shift the topic of conversation. At the rate they were headed, there was no way she could hold out until her divorce papers were signed.

"How about I tell you after they say yes. I can take you out tomorrow night to celebrate."

"OK." He wouldn't get any push back from her. Jason had the kids on Friday. It was a perfect idea.

"I gotta go look over some income statements and see if I can increase our profit margin."

"There you go," she said with her eyes closed. It affected her deeply when he spoke that way.

"I'm about to be knee-deep... in valuation." He used financial jargon, but he spoke it in the most erotic tone he could muster. Xavier usually said knee-deep when he described how far he would bury himself between her legs.

"I'll see you tomorrow, Zay."

"Damn, I can't wait."

The kids burst through the door the moment she disconnected the call. She continued to fan herself because of her body's response to the direction of her conversation with Xavier. Her divorce couldn't come fast enough.

Chapter Eleven

Xavier was a mess. He'd been in high-pressure situations before, but as he stood in front of the board of the Tinsville City Schools, doubt crept in about his ability to affect change at the level he desired. Everyone in the room, including Travis Gunther, the CEO, was at least a decade older than Xavier. They had life experience he didn't. Yet if they didn't make changes, the district's finances would continue to suffer.

"Alright, Grant. Robinson claims you have a solid solution to a problem that has stumped some of the most qualified officials in the region," Travis stated sarcastically.

Xavier respected Travis and the way he moved. Unlike him, Travis was well-versed at how to get people who didn't agree with him on his side. It was the type of finesse Xavier would be too conflicted to operate under. For him, finesse was a fancy word for manipulation. Xavier had a few seconds to choose his words carefully. He prayed his idea wouldn't come across as arrogant or land him in search of another job.

"The level of intelligence here is unquestionable. What I offer is an alternative and fresh perspective. I've been away from Tinsville for almost two decades, but my desire to see my city thrive hasn't changed."

"Spit it out, Grant. What do you propose we do?" Travis asked with his chin resting on his hands.

Xavier had his full attention, along with the rest of his colleagues.

"The Tinsville City Schools own this property near the airport." Xavier pulled up a bird's eye view of the vacant land. "It's miles from the school and isn't being used in any way. These acres are worth millions, and the location alone makes it highly sought after. If we sell it, we would not only have enough to pay the full amount of our debt, but we'd also have enough money to reinvest."

Whispers filled the space, and Xavier released the breath he'd held all week. Travis was stunned.

"If you approve this, Tinsville City Schools would undoubtedly make national news. I'm talking about published articles and an increase in visibility."

"I'll be damned," Richard muttered.

Xavier shot him a smile that he returned. "This kid might be onto something," he added.

Travis stood and rounded the large conference desk where Xavier stood. He patted him roughly on the back. "Good shit, Grant. Good shit!"

Destiny figured if she met Xavier at the restaurant, they would be less likely to end up at the other's house. After the way her prayers had been answered, she was committed to celibacy until she was legally single. Her children were with Jason for the weekend, and Xavier told her Zay J was with Simone. Should she mention how she'd unintentionally flirted with Jeff? It was innocent, but still too close for comfort.

Destiny sat at the bar and waited for her date. She was early and wanted to order a drink to calm her nerves before he arrived. While she was determined to wait to have sex, she still wanted to show Xavier what could be all his if he played his cards right. Destiny bought a dress from a boutique in the mall after her conversation with Zay. It was hidden beneath unreasonably priced garments and was marked clearance.

When Destiny tried the floor-length mesh maxi dress on, she smiled to herself. The outfit would drive her date wild. With her hair and makeup done, all eyes were on her. Her deep brown skin shimmered against the tan color of her dress. The restaurant Xavier chose was less than a mile from the Suite Seduction. She took a gulp of her drink as her mind drifted to their time at the lush hotel. Today was a new day, and a lot had changed since then.

"Dayum, Destiny."

Destiny craned her neck to see Xavier, who stood with his bottom lip tucked between his beautiful teeth. She wanted to put herself on display so he could see what was in store, but it seemed her plan may have backfired. Her eyes surveyed him from head to toe in his simple black slacks and his tailored Ivory button-up shirt. His clothes hugged his body just right. When she returned her gaze to his hazel eyes, he didn't try to hide his excited smirk.

He held his hand up to pull her to her feet. Xavier licked his lips when he saw her freshly manicured feet. He spun her around, unbothered by the other patrons.

"This is not fair. How am I supposed to keep my hands to myself when you wrapped yourself like the most salacious gift I've ever seen?"

She blushed. "I haven't been out in a while. I wanted to look nice."

Xavier's lips twisted to the side of his face. "I call bullshit, Dee Dee. You knew what you was doin' when you slipped this sexy shit on." His eyes raked over her body unhurriedly. "And your ass... I'm getting my shit straight in record timing."

"We'll see," Destiny added.

The bartender informed them that the hostess could seat them if they were ready. For the first time, Destiny made eye contact with a few of the other patrons. No one stood out, and she was relieved. They were fifteen minutes from Tinsville, but because the town was small, there was a good chance she could run into someone she knew. They were seated near a window that faced outdoors.

It was an intimate area of the swanky establishment, but there were tables outside that seemed even more romantic.

"I want to sit outside."

Xavier spoke to the hostess quietly, then discretely slid her money. They probably hadn't opened seats outdoors. Destiny watched as the waitress scurried over and arranged place settings at the table she selected. The breeze kissed her skin and helped to relax her frazzled nerves. Xavier moved like a boss. All she had to do was say what she wanted, and he made it happen.

He'd been that way with her when they were younger, only he didn't have the money he had now. Xavier was historically attentive with her. The only difference was they were no longer teens. He was a grown ass man. And although she'd been married for nineteen years, she was unaccustomed to someone who took charge. She was the alpha in her marriage. Not because she wanted to be, but out of necessity.

"You look beautiful, Destiny," Xavier said. His confession pulled her out of her deep contemplation.

"Thank you."

He chose to sit next to her instead of beside her, which was why the view of the water took her thoughts away from the present moment. The cedar and nutmeg scent he wore hypnotized her. She could feel Xavier's body heat because of his proximity.

"How did the meeting go?" She shifted to give him her full attention. His wide smile sent shivers up her spine. *Damn this man is fine!*

"It went amazing. Better than I could have planned."

"Tell me about it."

He reared his head back and furrowed his brows. "I know you

said investment words turn you on, but you really want to hear about my meeting?"

"They do get me hot under the collar." Destiny laughed lightly. "But that's not why I asked. I sincerely want to know. That's if you can tell me."

"I shouldn't, but I don't suspect you'll run to the Tinsville Times."

Destiny held onto his every word. Now that he wasn't upset with her and they weren't sleeping together, she could get to know the all-grown-up version of Xavier Grant. He was happy to discuss his work. It was as though he hadn't had a listening ear in far too long. Well, those times were done.

"Promise." Destiny held her pinky toward him, and he took it.

"Tinsville City Schools are twelve million dollars in debt."

"How is that possible?"

"I know. When Coach Archer said the former CFO was going to retire, he put my name in the hat for the position."

Destiny smiled at the sound of Donald Archer's name. He was a hard ass, but she remembered how much he meant to Xavier. Jace didn't get the pleasure of playing for him because he'd already retired. "How is he?"

"The same. I went to him when I was struggling last month."

"Oh." Destiny's shoulders sagged. Part of her was relieved he had someone he could go to for advice. Xavier mentioned he and Willie Earl made peace, but she doubted they spoke as casually as he did with his former coach.

Xavier rubbed the back of his head. "He slapped the shit out of me when he found out what we've been doing since he knows we're married to other people. He would be impressed with your bound-aries around waiting."

Destiny could only imagine a nearly seventy-year-old Donald slap Xavier.

"Anyway, I had the audacity to think I could add something of value to the district. Keep in mind, I'm at least a decade younger than everyone there."

"Really?"

"Yup. I took my time the first few weeks to show I could be a team player, and my intention wasn't to bulldoze the systems they built. But I decided when I interviewed that I would suggest they sell the land they own near the airport. The revenue from the sale will not only take the district out of debt, but there should also be money left over to invest."

Destiny squirmed in her seat. Xavier's mind was brilliant. Of course, his plan would work. He'd been in town for less than a summer, and he would change things for the better. His actions would positively affect Summer, Junior, and Zay J's future.

"Wow."

Xavier's eyes dropped to her breasts. The top of her dress featured a bustier style. The halter straps resembled a bra.

"Wow is right," Xavier said as he leaned in. "Can I kiss you if I keep my hands to myself?"

She nodded. He closed the distance between them and planted an unhurried kiss on her lips. Destiny couldn't help herself. She slipped her tongue into his mouth, and this time, he moaned. They separated when the hostess opened the door for another couple.

Destiny hadn't moved her attention from Xavier's lips until someone said her name.

"Destiny?" a deep voice asked. He was excited to greet her.

"Jeff?"

Xavier tightened beside her. *Oh, shit!*

* * *

Jeff and Simone stood next to Xavier's side of the table. The chill vibe the two of them created was gone. Not only was Xavier confused by the sight of Simone without their son, but he was furious at how familiar Jeff seemed with Destiny. *The hell?*

"Where's Zay J?" he asked through clenched teeth.

"Hello to you too, Xavier." The steam floated from Simone as she eye'd Destiny in the most orgasmic dress Tinsville and its surrounding areas had ever seen. Simone normally saw Destiny in sweats, and although it bothered her to discover she also had a child with Xavier, she'd underestimated how fine Destiny was. Xavier could practically read her thoughts.

"Where's our son?" he repeated.

Simone rolled her eyes at Destiny. "He's with your mother."

"How do you know Simone's husband, Destiny?" Jeff asked. This man still had no fucking idea how to read the room.

Xavier's eyes swung in Destiny's direction.

"I met Jeff at work," she mumbled to Xavier without a response to Jeff's inquiry.

Xavier inwardly counted to ten. He'd been to Destiny's job, the one with the ridiculously tempting lingerie. How the hell had she run across Jeff? And why the fuck did he have a smug smirk on his face as he appreciated the way her dress highlighted each of her curves?

"I was looking for a gift for Simone, and Destiny helped me pick it out," Jeff said. He hadn't taken his eyes off Destiny's body and Xavier's fists balled beneath the table.

Destiny's soft hand rest against his knee. His body calmed as he tried to wrap his head around what the hell happened.

"She likes the perfume, just like you said. Let her smell, babe." Jeff attempted to pull Simone's hand in their direction. "Destiny said it would smell different when it mixed with your body's natural scent. I learned a lot."

"You bought this from her?" Simone screeched. She snatched her hand back, crossed her arms, and rolled her eyes again.

"I work at the store where he bought the items. I had no idea—"

"I know that." Xavier wasn't sure who to be mad at. He wanted to believe Destiny hadn't flirted with Simone's Jeff. The guy was good-looking, but he was an idiot.

"I get the impression you two don't get along." Jeff stated the obvious as he swung his head between Simone and Destiny. "Oh." Jeff cupped his hands in front of his mouth. "She's the one with a baby by your husband!" he blurted.

Simone stormed back into the restaurant where the hostess nervously awaited the end to their awkward conversation.

"I should go. It was nice to see you again, Destiny," Jeff said with a little too much sincerity as far as Xavier was concerned. He reached his hand toward her but felt the heat from Xavier's glare. He wisely decided against it, then turned toward the door where Simone exited.

Silence stretched between their table, and as angry as Xavier was, he noticed Destiny fidget in her seat. How she could be turned on right now was beyond him. He almost broke Jeff's jaw.

"How long did you chat with Jeff for him to be that comfortable with you?"

Destiny's lips were tucked between her teeth, and she shifted for the third time since they were alone, but she said nothing.

"You like it when I'm jealous?"

Destiny nodded.

"How am I supposed to keep my hands to myself now?" Xavier swallowed. He was still pissed. Destiny was turned on. "I gotta see if you're wet. It's killing me not to reach under the table."

Destiny's eyes rolled in the back of her head. When she opened them, he watched as she shimmied her dress up to her knees. Xavier's throat went dry. Destiny put her hands between her legs and showed him the evidence of her juicy condition.

"Dayum!"

Xavier pulled out his phone.

"What are you doing?" Destiny's erotic tone had the ability to bring him to climax with minimal effort.

"I need to send an email to my lawyer."

"About what?"

"Expediting my divorce."

His head was buried in his phone as he drafted a quick message. By his calculations, the process shouldn't take much longer. Simone came into the marriage with little savings. Xavier was the one with all the assets. He wouldn't deny that they'd grown since he'd been with Simone.

Xavier was able to do his job at the level he did because she shouldered the daily responsibilities with taking care of his son and running their home. He would gladly give her half of everything, except for what he set aside for Zay J. Xavier wasn't worried about money. He could always make more. His concern was his relationship with his boys and the beautiful woman to his left. Xavier finished the email and tucked his phone away.

Destiny readjusted her dress and used a napkin to take care of the nectar—left on her hand—Xavier would pay money to drink. She was in her head again already. "This is what I was worried about. What if she makes things hard for you?"

"She won't."

"How do you know that? Did you see how she looked at me?"

Xavier pushed out a sigh. Destiny had a point. They all saw the envy in Simone's glare. She looked like she would strangle Destiny or burst into tears. He reacted the same way when Jeff had the nerve to let his eyes travel the length of Destiny's body. If Jeff wanted to be with Simone, that was fine, but Destiny was off limits.

"I did. But I told you, money's not an issue. That's the only way she can try to make me suffer."

"No, it's not."

"Maybe you're right. I'll talk to her when she drops Zay J off." Not wanting to waste another moment on things he couldn't control, Xavier focused on the present. "Did I tell you how good you look?"

"Yes." Destiny blushed. "Can you sit across from me though?"

"Why? What's wrong?"

"I can't concentrate when you're this close."

Xavier leaned in to invade her personal space. Her breath hitched when he did. He planted a slow, sensual kiss to her lips then stood to switch chairs.

"Now can we finish our date?"

"Yes." Destiny responded on an exhale.

"Tell me about your work."

Destiny threw her head to the side dramatically. "You really want to talk about this?"

"Yes. You know about mine. Plus, I want to get to know more than your grown-ass body."

"Is that right?"

"That's right. As much as I'm in agony over not touching you, it might be a blessing in disguise."

"How so?"

"I want to get to know you again. A lot has happened since I've been away. It would be hard to do with my face between..." Xavier didn't finish his sentence, just stared at her breasts.

"You are so silly." Her light laughter tickled his ears and made his chest tighten.

"Tell me about *Upundies*. And why would they name a sexy store something that sounds like a wedgie?"

Destiny burst into laughter.

"You know it does," he added as he watched the girl of his dreams finally relax.

"I've been there since high school. The incentives are top tier, and I never take advantage of people when I sell their products. Who doesn't want to feel sexy and confident in their body?"

Xavier nodded as he listened intently.

"I got my associate in business—"

"Congratulations, baby."

"Thank you." Destiny blushed.

"Is it okay if I call you baby?"

She nodded then went on, even though Xavier had her flustered. "It seemed like no one wanted to take a chance on a young mother, but my company saw me as an asset. They've given me reasonable hours and exceptional raises. And most recently. I got promoted to district manager."

Xavier smiled brightly. "I'm not surprised. You seemed in your element there. I didn't get to see you in action for long, but from what I observed—before I stormed in—you looked like you owned the place."

"Tell me about Summer and Junior," Xavier pressed.

"Really?" Destiny scrunched her nose and lips as though she couldn't believe he was interested.

"Yes, woman. I wanna know about your children. How old are they? What are they like?"

"Oh. Summer is fourteen. She goes to the same school as Zay J. She punched a girl in the face for taunting Jace about having a different dad."

Xavier almost choked on his water.

"I know. But otherwise, she's your typical sassy teenager who has a good heart but picks the wrong friends."

"And Jason Jr.?"

"He's so funny. When we told him about you, he thought it was the coolest thing ever. He told Jace if he had two dads, he'd never have any bullies."

"That's cute. I'd love to meet them. I mean, you know, whenever you and Coop were okay with it."

Destiny's eyes were wide.

"Sorry for the wait. What can I get the two of you to drink?"

Neither of them noticed they hadn't ordered. They were too preoccupied with each other. Once their drink requests were in, they continued to speak about family. Destiny never returned to his question to meet her children, and he didn't press the subject. If Jace got to meet Zay J, he was satisfied with that. Xavier filled her in on more about his mother and Wille Earl, and Destiny caught Xavier up on her time with her sister.

"Does she still think I'm never leaving my wife?"

"When I dropped her off at the airport, she told me to go for it."

"Really?"

"Yep. I guess she saw how intently I was focused on making sure the kids were OK and not wasting energy on ways to win you back. The big sister in her had to know my kids were good before she concerned herself with matters of my heart."

"I always liked Tiff."

They ordered and ate some of the best food Xavier had since he'd moved back to Tinsville. He learned a ton of things about Destiny he hadn't known and shared more about him and Xavier Jr. He walked her to her car and internally kicked himself for letting her meet him.

"Can I follow you to make sure you get there safely?"

"I could try to say no, but you live across the street."

He opened her door and watched as she got in. He didn't miss the second glances from both male and female patrons on their way out.

"I'll wait ten minutes if you say no. Then you'll have a little space."

"It's fine. Watch my car's ass if you please."

Xavier closed her door. "No sexy talk, woman."

On the drive home, Xavier prayed the entire way. He'd listened to a handful of sermons since Archer invited him to church, and each week, the sermon was relevant to his life. Last week, the pastor preached about delayed gratification. He said we could experience pleasure now, or bliss later. Xavier wanted bliss with Destiny. He craved her body, but his soul wanted her beside him for the rest of his life.

He thanked God for Destiny. He prayed that God would watch over her in this season of her life. And he shocked himself when he prayed for the strength to leave her alone if they weren't healthy for each other. They were on their block in no time. Xavier ended his prayer, pleading for the restraint to keep his hands to himself.

Another thing he loved about the pastor of First Baptist was how approachable he was. He didn't make God sound like Xavier needed to be perfect or have the bible memorized to pray. In fact, Xavier was encouraged to pray about everything, like he would confide in a trusted friend. From then on, Xavier referred to God as G in his prayers.

You know how sexy she looks tonight. Help me keep my mind from fantasies about how good she feels. Help me to not be a creep and drool all over her. But please, let these divorces be final soon. I'm too old for blue balls. Thanks, G!

Xavier parked his car in front of Destiny's house, while she sat in her driveway. He exited his vehicle and hustled in her direction before she could get out.

"Can I sit inside?"

"Sure." She shrugged when she responded, and the movement of her titties made Xavier consider if the wise thing would be to call it a night.

G, why you make her look this fine? To torture me? Delayed gratification. Got it.

"I gotta ask you something, and I want you to be honest."

"OK."

"Is Jeff attractive?"

Destiny fell into a fit of laughter.

"He looks funny as hell, but I'm not a female."

"Honestly?"

"Yes, woman."

"He's not unattractive. He's kind of charming. We spent maybe fifteen minutes in conversation before he said his name. Then he left. I had no idea he was... you know."

Xavier hummed. He was jealous that Destiny found another man attractive, although it was completely unreasonable. He accepted she had two other kids and an eighteen-year marriage to his friend. Yet, somehow, an innocent interaction with Jeff still got him riled.

"There is this other guy," she started.

What the hell had he done? Did Destiny think they were homegirls?

He nodded and fought to keep himself calm.

"He's tall, and his body..." She moaned her appreciation. "Every woman in town fawns over him because he's the hottest guy in Tinsville."

"Destiny, I don't think—"

"And his eyes." She smirked in his direction when realization covered his chiseled features.

"Me?" He rested his hand on his chest.

"Yep. And none of those bitches can have you."

"Why not?" He turned in his seat to face her. They couldn't cross the line, but he could make out with her if she let him. They'd done that for months—when they were younger—before they went all the way.

Destiny grabbed his shirt and pulled him closer. "Because you're mine, right?"

He nodded, then kissed her to seal his admission. *G, help!*

Chapter Twelve

Xavier was grateful to be at another church service. He invited Simone and told her she could bring Jeff, but she declined. She hadn't mentioned their run in at dinner, and he decided to wait until they had more time to bring it up. Zay J bounced in his seat, eager for the young adult dismissal.

"Church hasn't even started, man. You look like you're gonna burst."

"Luna said she wants to hold my hand during prayer today."

Xavier swallowed his laughter. He wanted open communication with his son. If his dad made fun of him, Zay J would shut down.

"Is she nice?"

"Dad, she's the cutest girl I've ever seen."

Xavier smiled. "That's important. But it's also important that she's a nice girl."

Zay J rolled his eyes. "She told me to be quiet when I was talking while the youth pastor taught last week. Is that nice enough?"

This time, Xavier did laugh. "Yes, it is. Are you worried?"

"Heck yeah. What if my hand gets sweaty?"

"Just tell her the truth. If you say sometimes my hand gets sweaty and admit it's kind of embarrassing, a girl like that will understand."

"Thanks, Dad."

"Can we sit with you?"

Xavier and Zay J looked up to see Destiny and Jace at the end of their pew. Xavier nodded. He was speechless. *What is she doing here?*

He stood and motioned for Zay J to stand as well.

"Zay J, this is Destiny. And this is your brother, Jace."

Zay J's golden complexion reddened. "Really?"

"Yeah, man," Jace said as he stepped in the row and pulled Zay J in for a hug. Xavier's heart leaped, and he feared it would beat right out of his chest he was so grateful.

"It's super good to meet you," Zay J said when he pulled back. "How old are you?" he asked with little concern for his volume.

"I'm eighteen."

"This is Jace's mom, Destiny," Xavier added.

Jace stepped further in the aisle so Zay J and Destiny could meet. When he did, he said, "Hey," to Xavier. He wasn't sure what Jace would call him, but the fact that he leaned in for a hug was plenty.

"You look prettier than Luna," Zay J said as he stared up at Destiny.

"That's enough," Xavier said and pulled his mini me back toward him.

"Don't tell my mom," he added with embarrassment etched on his youthful features.

"I wouldn't dare," Destiny said with a wink.

"Your mom likes me," Zay J said and elbowed Jace.

Jace shook his head and took a seat beside Zay J, with them in the middle and their parents on the opposite sides of them.

The sermon started, and Xavier couldn't focus. Every few moments, his eyes would drift toward Destiny. Then he'd look at his boys, and his heart would flutter. Would Summer and Junior ever come? He would like that.

The music began, and when they stood, Zay J whisper yelled, "You like my brother's mom... again?"

Xavier studied his face. Somehow, he didn't seem bothered.

"What if I said I do?"

"I'd say okay." He shrugged. "Besides, Mom has Jeff."

Xavier literally bit the inside of his cheek. How the hell did Zay J know about Jeff? They would need to discuss how they introduced people to their child.

Xavier was distracted for most of the praise and worship songs. Could he handle all that starting two new families would entail? Would Destiny's other children feel left out? Would they like him? How about Simone? Would she want Zay J around Destiny?

The music ended, and the young people were dismissed. Like he did every time, Xavier grabbed the bottom of Zay J's shirt.

"I know, Dad. It's creepy people everywhere. I have my phone."

Destiny covered her mouth to hide her giggle.

"I can look out for him," Jace said, shocking both of his parents.

"Thank you, Jace," Destiny added.

Xavier watched as Jace walked with Zay J toward the back of the sanctuary. Zay J pointed out Luna to him as they disappeared behind the closed doors.

Xavier closed the space between him and Destiny where the kids had been. He noticed that neither of them had worn their rings since she agreed to go out with him on Friday, and it brought a smile to his face. Destiny leaned into him as the pastor began the service. As if G knew he needed confirmation, the title of the sermon was 'what man says is the right thing versus what God says is right'.

Throughout church, Xavier watched as Destiny took notes. He found it endearing and attractive. He could picture the two of them here every week. They honored God by waiting to have sex, and therefore, Xavier prayed things with Jason and Simone would end smoothly.

After service, Xavier was anxious to get to his boys. He hoped things had gone well for them. But every time he and Destiny made it a few steps, someone would stop her to say hello. Most of them were nosy and simply wanted to see up close if the rumors were true, but a few of them showed genuine concern.

"It's so nice to see you, Destiny. How is Jason? How are the kids?" an older woman asked.

"They all are fine," Destiny replied.

Xavier wished she'd tell the old bat it was none of her business, but it wasn't in Destiny's nature.

"I see you're not wearing your ring, and you brought a visitor."

The hell?

"Mrs. Sanders, this is Xavier Grant. Do you remember him?" Destiny pulled Xavier until he stood beside her.

"This Constance Grant's boy?"

"I am."

"Welcome back. She must be so happy you're home."

Xavier gave her a cordial nod. "Can you excuse us?"

"I can. But just be sure you close one door before you open another one. Understand?"

He did. These people needed to mind their damn business. In place of a verbal response, Xavier guided Destiny away with his hand resting on the small of her back. They were almost out of the doors when someone called his name.

"Grant."

This is just what I need!

Destiny gently yanked on his shirt. "Are you okay?"

"Hey, Coach," Xavier said. "Mrs. Archer."

Coach Archer's wife pinned Xavier and Destiny with accusatory glares of disgust, then walked away.

"Hello, Coach Archer," Destiny said. She was flustered from the abrupt way his wife walked off.

"Hello, Destiny. How's the family?"

"We're great," she said with forced enthusiasm. "Not sure if you heard, but Jason moved out and has a steady girlfriend. When we were together, they came and went so much, I never knew who was who. Our separation is legally official, and we've started the divorce process with mediation. Also, Jace just met his brother. They're downstairs! And I'm starting to get used to being the only adult in my home each night with two of my children. Is that what you mean when you say, 'how's the family'?"

Destiny didn't wait for his response. Several nearby church ladies fanned themselves as they got the earful Destiny doled out to Coach. Xavier respected him, but there was judgment in his tone when he spoke to her.

"I value your opinion, Coach. You know that. But what you just did was foul." Xavier pushed through the crowd to catch up with Destiny.

"Can we please leave?"

"Of course. What can I do?" It was dumb for him to think the congregation would openly receive two people seated together who were in marriages with other people.

"Take me to my... our son."

Xavier nodded and walked her to the gym. When they stepped in, they saw something that completely made up for the end of service drama. Jace and Zay J's church clothes were drenched. Jace showed Zay J how to do a crossover. Destiny clapped her hand over her mouth. He noted the tears well in her eyes.

"I'm so glad I didn't ruin this," she said about Jace's relationship with his brother.

"If only we could be as resilient as our kids."

A young girl, who put him in the mind of a teenage Destiny, walked up to the court where the boys were and said goodbye. In a move that caught Xavier completely off guard, Zay J leaned in for a hug, sweaty and all.

"He is quite the charmer," Destiny noted.

"He gets it honest, doesn't he?" Xavier flirted. "I'm sorry about all that back there."

"It's not your fault. I shouldn't have been disrespectful to your coach."

"I get it. I told him he was out of line."

"Dad," Zay J called out.

"Yeah, son."

"Can Destiny and Jace come with us to eat after church?"

Xavier hesitated. With as small as Tinsville was, an after church food outing could show up on the news. It didn't matter to him, but what happened to his kids and Destiny meant everything to him.

"What do you say?" he asked her.

* * *

What the hell was I thinking? The moment the four of them entered the diner, Destiny immediately regretted it. She incorrectly assumed since they didn't pick the unofficially designated 'after church' eatery, they could fly under the radar. *Wrong!* The first person Destiny saw was Constance Grant. And she did not look pleased.

As long as she didn't disrespect Jace, Destiny would keep her mouth shut.

"Do you want to go somewhere else?"

It was as if Xavier could read her thoughts.

Destiny shook her head. This wouldn't be the first and it certainly wouldn't be the last time someone would criticize her for her choices. She had no intention of moving out of Tinsville. And since she also intended to be with Xavier, in whatever capacity she could, there would be plenty of bullies and naysayers like his mother.

Constance wore a mean mug as she made her way toward Destiny. It changed when Zay J waved.

"Hey, grandma's baby." She used a syrupy sweet voice like she wasn't evil personified.

Destiny rolled her eyes. Constance didn't like her, but never in a million years did she think she was capable of the devilish lies she'd told. Nineteen years ago, when Destiny was pregnant with Jace, Constance convinced her that Xavier left for school early. Meanwhile, Xavier believed Destiny suddenly had no interest in seeing him off. She wouldn't call her on her shit today, but Destiny drew the line when it came to Jace. She would be damned if her future monster-in-law made him feel unwanted.

Zay J accepted his grandmother's bear hug.

"Mimi. This is my brother, Jace."

Jace looked to Xavier who nodded. "This is my mom."

"It's nice to meet you," Jace said with his hand outstretched.

Constance glared at Destiny one last time, then faced Jace. It was as though it was the first time she'd given herself permission to take him in. Her steely demeanor melted. Destiny recognized the expression on her oldest son's face. He'd given his paternal grandmother the same charm Xavier used when he wanted his way. Jace recognized her hesitation and refused to let her deny him—his hazel eyes bore into her soul.

Constance pushed his extended hand aside and pulled him in for a hug.

"You look just like your father."

The patrons in the restaurant continued to mind their business. They'd barely stopped their meals at all. Constance abandoned her group of friends to sit with Destiny, Xavier, and the boys.

"Have they met your father?" Constance asked Xavier when everyone was seated.

"I don't know my dad's dad," Zay J piped up.

"Me either," Jace told Zay J. The smile they shared warmed Destiny's heart.

"No, they haven't. They're meeting you first, Mom." Xavier gritted his teeth in response to the smug look his mother wore. It was another leg up for her when it came to Willie Earl. Xavier never spoke of him until his return to Tinsville, and her inability to let go was why.

Everything went well at lunch between Jace and Xavier's mother. Jace had met Zay J and Constance for the first time, but you certainly couldn't tell. They acted as though they had been around each other for years. *Maybe it's because Jace's mannerisms are just like Xavier's. She couldn't reject him if she tried.*

Her phone buzzed as they waited for the boys' dessert.

Xavier Grant: Are you okay?

Destiny: Yes. Thank you for asking.

Xavier Grant: I'm trying to date you

Destiny's cheeks flushed. She recalled that the first time he said he wanted to date her was in high school. She had a thing for Xavier the moment she laid eyes on him, but when he finally approached her, she was a goner. For months, she had a permanent smile plastered on her face. Destiny never had many friends, but she confided in Tiffany, who made fun of her lovesick behavior.

When she tore her gaze from her phone, she found Xavier's hazel eyes locked on her appreciatively.

"Destiny," Constance blurted.

"Yes."

"Where's your husband?"

"Where's yours?" Destiny retorted.

Xavier choked on his water. "Hey, boys. Why don't you see if they have any trap music on the jukebox."

"A what?" Zay J asked with his face contorted. "Is that something people born in the late nineteen hundreds used?"

"I'll show you, man," Jace said with a chuckle. He was old enough to read the room, unlike his younger brother. Destiny made sure he was well-versed on grown folks' business.

"Mom—"

"No, Xavier. I got this one."

Destiny may have spent most of her life in avoidance of uncomfortable conversations. It was much more comfortable for her to run from anything close to conflict. But today was a new day. She fully accepted accountability for her choices. Somehow, she'd strengthened her muscle for the tricky things, and Constance would think twice before she fixed her lips to throw shade after Destiny finished with her. Her back was erect, and her gaze hadn't wavered.

"My husband lives in an apartment with his girlfriend. But I have a feeling you don't care. What I want to know is why you thought you had the right to lie to me about Xavier's leaving for school?"

"Little girl, I don't owe you shit," Constance spat.

"Mom—" Xavier attempted.

"You know what? It doesn't matter. Jace knows his father and his brother. No matter how hard you tried to keep us apart, it didn't work."

Constance narrowed her eyes. "And where is your wife, son?"

Destiny didn't wait for Xavier's response. Instead, she responded, "Simone's with Jeff."

Constance gasped. "Zav baby, you're going to let her talk to me like this?"

"I love you, Mama. But I told you weeks ago, I still love her."

Xavier winked at Destiny, which caused her to blush.

"I'm not going to pretend like everything is going to go smoothly, but I promise you, as soon as I get the paperwork back from my lawyer, I'm marrying Destiny." He grabbed Destiny's hand and stood. "Your ass should have been a Grant from the beginning," he said to Destiny.

"I hope you come to your senses soon, Mama. Jace is about to leave for college, and Zay J isn't getting any younger. I'll talk to you later."

With that, they found the boys and left his mother seated in disbelief.

* * *

Destiny and Xavier had two great weeks together after their run in with his mother. He'd been able to take Jace and Zay J to lunch now that school was officially out, and he'd even met Summer and Junior. Junior was as cute in person as he sounded when Destiny spoke of him. Summer was a little standoffish, but that was to be expected. The two of them looked so much like Coop it was unnerving.

The following week, Destiny was distant. Xavier was perplexed because she told him her divorce was final. Things should be easier now that she was legally single. When he pressed her about it, she asked for space. It was a stark contrast to the positive feedback he got on the job. There were several buyers who already placed bids on the property. The school district would wait for the best offer, and he would make Tinsville history.

Although he and Simone had come to an understanding financially, they couldn't agree on how the custody should be spelled out on paper. Simone wanted to move away from Tinsville. He not only respected her wishes, but he also supported her. But he wanted a specific mileage included in the separation so he wouldn't miss time with Zay J. Unfortunately, the idea of having a mileage limit made her feel micromanaged.

On top of everything, it was August first. Jace was set to move and begin school in a little over a month. Xavier wanted to squeeze a lifetime of memories into a short period of time. He'd been so obvious that Jace reminded him he wasn't moving out of the country. With that relationship in a good place, his divorce pending, and his job thriving, he wanted to focus all his energy on Destiny. His body and soul ached for her.

People at church asked about her when she stopped going. The word had gotten out about her divorce and the truth about their marriages. If he could only come to her with something concrete. He wanted more than her body and a few dates. Xavier wanted his Dee Dee permanently. His lawyer was positive that if he and Simone could agree on custody, they would be granted a divorce immediately.

Xavier: Can we try one last time?

Simone: I don't want to be controlled just because we broke up and you make all the money

Xavier: I know. What if I bought you a house here and somewhere closeish? You can live wherever the hell you want, but when Zay J is with you, you stay in one of those locations that's close enough for me to get to you if anything happens

Simone: I'll think about it

Xavier: Thank God

Simone: I didn't say yes, Xavier

Xavier: You didn't say no

Simone: Lol. Jeff says hi *sweating laughing emoji

Xavier: Really?!?

Simone: Yep! Give me a day or two to think about it

Xavier: I appreciate it

Simone: Of course. I know you want to be free of me

Xavier: *sweating laughing emoji

Simone: It's not my place... but your girl looks a mess. What did you do?

Xavier: It's not. But since you're my baby mama, and Jeff is my boy *rolling eyes emoji *her divorce is final, and I guess it hit her hard*

Simone: Yikes. Couldn't be me. I'm throwing one of those Instaglam divorce parties

Xavier: I bet you are. Get off my phone

Simone: Don't let her slip too far down the rabbit hole. She probably feels like she failed. From what Jeff says, her ex has been outside long before his current girlfriend. Work your Xavier magic and you two will skip off into the sunset

Xavier: I hope so. Later, Simone

Simone: Later

Xavier paced the floor. Zay J was asleep, and Destiny was home. He wasn't a stalker, but he'd tracker when she made it home each night. Maybe he was a stalker.

Xavier: I miss you

Destiny: I know

Well damn.

Xavier: Can I see you?

Destiny: Are you still married?

An email came through from Xavier's lawyer. He opened it and read it quickly.

Grant,

I'm not sure what you said to Simone, but she reached out to her lawyer and said she agrees to reside in the homes you promised when she's with Xavier Jr. as long as she can live wherever she wants. Official paperwork will be ready for the two of you to sign tomorrow.

Johnson

Excitement coursed through Xavier's body. The church lady said not to open a door before he closed the other. Well, it was closed as far as he was concerned. He couldn't wait any longer. He dialed Destiny's number and prayed she would pick up.

"Hey," Destiny said.

"Did I catch you at a bad time?"

"No. Summer is in her room, and Junior is asleep."

He didn't like how sad she sounded. He could help her heal if she let him in.

"I pray about you every day, Destiny."

She gasped quietly, but said nothing.

"I imagine this is hard for you. But don't shut me out, baby. Please."

"We said we'd wait until both of our divorces were final."

"To have sex. Not to spend time together. I miss you so bad it hurts."

"Oh."

"Don't you know that?"

"I..."

"The holdup was custody stuff with how far Simone could move. But we settled it."

"How? Can she move Zay J?"

"I bought her two houses?"

Destiny released a deep belly laugh. "You what?"

"I was desperate. I want my son and his mother close, and I want you. So I offered to buy her a home here and another home within a reasonable amount of miles. When she has my son, she needs to stay in one of those. When she doesn't, she can live wherever the hell she wants."

"Wow."

"What?"

"I think I love you," Destiny said quietly.

Xavier's chest tightened. Had he hallucinated? "What, baby? I didn't hear you."

"Yeah, you did."

"Say it to my face."

"OK."

She rustled around. He walked to his front window that faced her house. She stepped out on her porch with a robe, a bonnet, and her cell phone. With a huge grin on his face, he walked out of his home and locked his son in.

When he was in front of her, she gazed up at him and said, "I love you, Xavier Grant."

"Damn."

He pulled her in for a hug and prayed she'd never let go.

Chapter Thirteen

"Whose fuckin' pussy is this?"

"Zay!"

"Nah, I wanna hear you say it's mine. Whose pussy is this?"

"Yours," Destiny whined. "It's your pussy, Zay."

Her face full of freshly done makeup was pressed against the bathroom mirror as Xavier plunged into her flesh repeatedly.

"I thought we were going to wait until we got married," she whined.

"I said I would wait until you and I were single." Xavier removed his grip from the side of her face and used his hands to steady her round hips.

Destiny moaned. It was three short weeks after he showed up at her house to hear her say she loved him in person. It was also their wedding day, but Xavier couldn't hold off any longer. He'd stumbled across her bag for the evening. They would get married at the courthouse and have a reception in the backyard of their new home. Destiny was floored when Xavier told her the property and land where they would live had been a gift from Wille

Earl. He said Xavier already had too many mortgages for his ex-wife.

Destiny packed the bag because they were set to stay a week at the Suite Seduction since neither of them wanted to be far from the kids. He had no business in her bag, but apparently, he found the throat numbing spray she packed for their time away as newlyweds. When he cornered her in the bathroom and confronted her about it, she shrugged. She reminded him that the marriage bed couldn't be defiled. Xavier lost his last shred of restraint and took her right there.

"The hell you buy that spray for?"

"You know why," Destiny teased.

"You trying to take me deep in your throat?"

Destiny nodded. She loved how freaky Xavier spoke to her, but she could barely concentrate on his next stroke let alone form words to respond. The sensations that swam through her threatened to obliterate her sanity.

"Yes!"

They had an hour before they were scheduled to arrive for their nuptials. She begged him for a small wedding, and he relented. His compromise was that they'd have a reception with their friends and family.

Her cream robe was hiked up because Xavier hadn't bothered to remove it.

"I been waiting for you, Dee Dee."

She peered at his reflection in the mirror and found his eyes locked on hers.

"You know that?"

She nodded. Xavier slowed down his strokes but gripped her cheeks and went deeper. Destiny moaned her appreciation. It was the most pleasurable pain she'd ever experienced.

"I prayed and fasted for you because I didn't know another way to honor your request to wait for sex. The last time we made love wasn't enough. All it did was show me what I want to enjoy for the rest of my life."

Tears sprang to her eyes as his words registered. *He prayed for me?*

"I wanted you the moment I was single. I couldn't wait for you to take my last name."

Xavier withdrew from her, and she whined in protest.

"I need to see your face," he continued. He lifted her and pressed her back against the wall. "Tell me your name."

"Destiny Davis."

Xavier smiled. "Your new last name, baby."

"Destiny Grant."

His pace became frenzied. "Say it again."

"Destiny Grant."

"You fuckin' right."

Destiny's body tensed, and waves of pleasure tore through her violently. She had been wound up since the first time Xavier reacquainted himself with her body at the beginning of the summer. She vowed not to sleep with him again until they were single. It was one of the most difficult decisions to stick by with the way in which he courted her. He'd forgiven her and been a present and amazing father to both of his children.

When she opened her eyes, hypnotic hazel eyes pierced hers. Two strokes later, and Xavier released a throaty groan as he filled her with his essence.

"Can we get married now?"

"Hell yeah."

"I guess we already took care of the consummation part."

"No, the hell we didn't. That was a preview. You ain't seen nothing yet, Mrs. Grant."

He separated from her and slapped her ass roughly. Any nerves Destiny had about the court nuptials were replaced with immense pleasure and physical aftershocks of Mr. Grant's hard work. The throat numbing spray had been a gift from the girls at her job. Thank God, she kept it.

It didn't take Destiny long to get dressed and touch up her

makeup once Xavier agreed to leave her be. The only people in the courtroom were Destiny, Xavier, Jace, Zay J, Tiffany, and Willie Earl. Everyone else would join them at the reception. The judge was an older man with kind eyes. He insisted it didn't matter where a marriage certificate was signed if there was the type of love and commitment he saw between Destiny and Xavier.

"Have you had counseling?" Judge Mason asked as everyone filtered in.

"Pastor Dent from First Baptist did our premarital sessions with us," Xavier said with his chest puffed out.

"Pastor Dent's a good man. If he gave you his blessing, I'm sure the two of you will be fine. Dent asks hard questions, but that's only so your names don't appear in the courts again."

Pastor Dent had asked hard questions. One of their worst arguments to date was when Destiny confessed her fear that Xavier may still be angry with her about keeping Jace from him. Xavier was adamant that he'd moved beyond it, but when Destiny admitted she wasn't sure she was confident that he wouldn't get upset with her again in the future, he lost it. Pastor Dent helped Xavier translate his reaction to Destiny's concerns and how her hesitation contradicted his desire for her total trust.

They worked through it and were confident they had the tools to navigate their past, present, and future. Pastor Dent pleaded with them to wait at least six more months since they were both newly divorced—but of course, they refused. Dent informed the couple that their haste was his only concern and otherwise they had his blessing.

Judge Mason directed everyone to their places and the ceremony began.

"Thank you all for coming to witness the union between Xavier Amore Grant and Destiny Elizabeth Davis," the judge said to those in attendance.

He shifted his gaze to Destiny and Xavier. "You two have willingly decided to take a sacred rite of passage that will bind you to the other in body, mind, and soul."

"Ick," Zay J said under his breath. Only the poor thing had no idea how to whisper so everyone heard him.

"Give it time, son. You'll change your mind," Willie Earl added.

"Xavier Grant. Do you take—"

"I do." Xavier admired Destiny with little regard for the Judge or anyone else in attendance.

"I appreciate your enthusiasm, but let me finish my statement before you sign a verbal contract," Mason urged.

"Xavier Grant, do you take Destiny Elizabeth Davis to be your spiritual and lawful partner in the eyes of God and the state? Do you promise to love her beyond her faults, exercise forgiveness, and protect and support her to the best of your abilities?"

"I still do," Xavier said. It earned him a few snickers from Tiffany, Jace, and Willie Earl.

"Destiny Davis, do you take—"

"Judge Mason?"

"Yes, dear." Judge Mason's shoulders sagged. It seemed they wouldn't allow the poor man to read his script so he could be on his way.

"Is it okay if I speak my vows from my heart?"

"Go ahead."

Destiny blew out a breath. "Xavier, I have loved you since the first time I laid eyes on you. But life was lifeing, and we lost touch. We made life," she said and looked in Jace's direction. He gave her an encouraging nod. "But I kept it from you. I know you are a gift from God because you forgave me. You want the best for me. And I believe you'd move heaven and earth for me if it came to that."

Xavier's jovial demeanor turned serious. He hung on her every word.

"You are a phenomenal father and an overall dope human being. When you reentered my life, my faith in God was restored. For the rest of my life, I will love and honor God and you. I'm so grateful I get to raise our kids together and do life with you. I love you always."

Xavier leaned forward and pulled her into a deep kiss.

"Man, you know we're not at that part yet," Judge Mason said with irritation in his voice.

Xavier pulled back with his eyes still locked on his bride. "I'm sorry, Judge. I couldn't help myself. When the prettiest girl in the world says she loves me, you can't blame a brotha for needing to kiss her."

"Mr. Grant, do you have rings?"

Jace presented two rings. He gave one to his mother, who pulled him into a hug. "I love you, Jace."

"Love you too, Mom."

And he gave the second to Xavier who slapped the back of his hand, then the front, and gripped him up in a handshake Destiny had never seen. Xavier hadn't given Destiny a ring when he proposed, and she was fine with it. They had so much history together and were much more aware of what was important. But when she saw the intricate diamond engagement ring soldered to an equally breathtaking wedding band, her bottom lip trembled.

"What did you do?" she whispered.

"I finally got my girl. I need the whole fucking world to see," Xavier said with a wink.

"Ugh," Zay J added. "This is so gross."

"He don't be saying all that to Luna," Jace teased.

"That's different. Luna is fine."

Judge Mason cleared his throat. "Xavier, place the ring on Destiny's finger and repeat after me. Let this ring symbolize my love. Let it represent our past, present, and our future."

"Dee Dee, let this expensive ass ring symbolize my love. Let it represent the first time I got it, this morning, and all the times I'll get it down the line."

"Ugh," Jace and Zay J sang.

"I'm with them on this one. Nobody wants to hear all that," Tiff added in disgust.

"I'm sorry. I can't help it," Xavier offered.

"Destiny, place the ring on Xavier's finger and repeat after me.

Let this ring symbolize my love. Let it represent our past, present, and our future."

"Zay, let this ring symbolize my love. Let it represent our past, present, and our future."

"By the authority vested in me, I now pronounce you husband and wife. Xavier, you may kiss your wife... again."

Xavier didn't hold back his excitement. He kissed her, then lifted her from her feet.

* * *

Xavier was on cloud nine. Destiny was officially Destiny Grant. All was well in his world. His sons were happy, and he and his dad had a better relationship. His new home was charming and big enough to house all four of the kids. Coop and Simone had been there several times since their children would be there at least half the time. It hadn't been the smoothest of transitions, but he was confident things would fall into place with time.

The wedding planner Destiny hired decorated the backyard for the reception. The lights added an intimate touch for the pending sunset. Simone and Jeff were seated near Coop and his girlfriend, Jasmine. The kids were seated at a table next to Coop's divorced parents. They seemed to get along well. Xavier prayed his new blended family could behave as respectfully as they did.

Coop's parents treated Zay J like one of their own. He blossomed from his larger family. Xavier's mother showed up to the reception late. If she expected anyone to be mad or break their necks to greet her, she was sorely mistaken. She had the nerve to be upset at how much Wille Earl was involved and she wasn't.

Of course, her knee jerk reaction was to blame Destiny, but Xavier set her straight. Coach Archer hadn't approved of the way they started, yet Destiny called him personally to make amends and invite him for Xavier's sake. He came without his wife, and that was just fine.

"Mimi, come meet my new bonus brother and sister," Zay J said. He was always excited to see his grandparents.

She mumbled under her breath but agreed to say hello to Junior and Summer.

A clink on Tiffany's glass alerted everyone that it was time for speeches.

"My sister knows I hate Tinsville."

Hushed laughter echoed from guests at a few tables.

"So, I'm rarely here. When I came back this summer, I was worried about Destiny. Her world had turned upside down, and she didn't have Mom to help her through it."

Destiny sniffled, and Xavier pulled her into his shoulder.

"I came and saw my baby sister pick herself up and get her house in order. I always loved her, but for one of the first times, I was deeply proud of the way she took responsibility for herself.

Now that she has Xavier, I don't have to worry about her heart. He has shown that he's patient and capable of forgiveness. I love him for you, sis. And I look forward to y'all coming to visit me because I still hate Tinsville."

Despite his mother's evil ways, Destiny planned a mother and groom dance since her father wasn't there. Xavier wasn't thrilled about it but relented.

"I see you're trying to make up for not including me," she said as they danced to Boyz II Men's song "Mama".

"I'm not. This was Destiny's idea. She said you might feel left out now that I have a relationship with Willie Earl."

She kissed her teeth. "I don't know how he afforded this house with all the kids he has."

"You still haven't let it go. You can't say one nice thing?"

"What do you want me to say, Zavy baby." I don't like Destiny for you. And she has her ex-husband and their kids here. It's ghetto and you're better than this."

Xavier released her. "Would it kill you to be happy for me? To support me even though you disagree. How about tell me you're glad to see me?"

She opened her mouth, but Xavier wasn't finished. "And I love those kids. I'm going to raise them like they're mine. You wanna know why I keep in touch with Willie Earl all of a sudden?"

She shrugged.

"Because he knows how to parent adult children. He may have missed out on a lot when I was younger, but he's here now. Where are you, Mama?"

Xavier stepped off the glass dance floor atop the grass and stopped only when Destiny caught up to him.

"You OK?" She asked sweetly.

"I love you." He leaned in and planted a kiss to his wife's lips.

"I know, baby. But are you OK?"

"I think so. She's never going to change. And it took today for me to accept that."

Destiny leaned up and hugged him. He had no idea how much he needed it until she did.

* * *

"Hey, Mom."

Destiny spun around to see Jace with his hand outstretched.

"I know your dad isn't here for the father and bride dance. Do you want to dance with me instead?" Destiny's eyes welled with fresh tears. She'd redone her makeup at least three times.

She looked at Xavier who smiled. "Bring her back when you're done."

"You got it, boss."

Jace was a mirror image of his father. He'd been taller than her for some time, but in the last month that he'd lived with Jason's father, he'd changed. He was bigger and wiser.

"You look pretty, Mama," Jace said as they swayed.

"Thank you, son. You do too."

"I'm handsome, not pretty."

"With those eyes, you better get used to it."

"I know I've said it a million times, but I'm gonna miss you when you leave."

"About that..."

"What's the matter?"

"Nothing, we'll talk later."

They ended the dance with a hug, and Destiny invited everyone to the dance floor. The reception was just about over when Destiny noticed a girl she didn't recognize with Jace.

"Who's that?" Destiny whispered to Xavier.

"Jace's girlfriend, Bliss."

Destiny craned her neck up to see him.

"You got one more time to whisper close to my ear like that and I'm saying fuck this party."

Destiny rolled her eyes.

"You trying to have a bathroom repeat?"

She swatted his arm. "I'm serious. What the hell kind of name is Bliss? Sounds like a stripper."

Before Xavier could respond, Destiny marched in their direction.

"Mom, this is my girlfriend, Bliss."

Destiny couldn't hide her frown. *Who is this little girl? And why is she at my wedding? In that skimpy dress no less!*

"Bliss, this is my mom."

"Oh my gosh. Ms. Destiny, you are such a beautiful bride. I love your home."

Destiny eyed the girl from head to toe. Before she could speak, Xavier's heat was behind her. "Be nice, baby," he whispered in her ear.

"They are so freakin' cute," Bliss said as she elbowed Jace. He, on the other hand, looked like he wanted to be sick whenever he caught their PDA.

"What school are you going to?" Destiny asked. She could try to give the heifer a chance.

"I'm going to the community college. Jace said you went there too."

"I did. But that's because I was pregnant with Jace and couldn't go away to a four-year school like Xavier did and Jace plans to." Destiny's eyes bulged. "Wait, are you pregnant?"

"Mom!" Jace yelled.

"No. I mean, I don't think so. Let me check my app."

Jace's cheeks reddened.

Destiny swirled in place to face Xavier. "What did she say? Did this heffa just say what I think she said?"

"Baby, I know it's hard, but Jace is an adult. Surely you knew he's sexually active," Xavier whispered so only she could hear.

"I accept this in my head, but does she have to be so flippant?"

"Nope. I'm right on schedule. But Jace isn't going to a four-year school."

Destiny almost blacked out. "What?"

"Well, Bliss and I figured we could save money if we get an apartment together and take our general education classes locally, then we'll transfer to a four-year school. That way we don't go into debt paying for overpriced classes and housing."

"They not wrong about the sticker price for school, babe," Xavier added, but closed his mouth when Destiny glared at him.

"You're supposed to leave in a week," she said to Jace.

Constance ambled in Destiny's direction. "This is exactly how I felt. Xavier was Jace's age and in love with you. You better than me? Then give him your blessing."

Destiny gritted her teeth. It was her wedding day for God's sake. She was ready to start her honeymoon and now this. *God, am I being like my wench of a mother-in-law? Am I supposed to support Jace in making a decision he's too young for?*

Destiny's prayers seemed to be answered immediately. What might have happened had Constance not meddled in her and Xavier's young love. She didn't regret their children with other people, but they suffered unnecessarily because of his mother.

Destiny blew out a breath. "Bliss, this is a lot for me to take in. It's the first I'm hearing of it. How about we all sit down next week after Xavier and I are back from our honeymoon?"

"Ayyyye," Bliss said. She bopped around and twerked on Jace but stood when she saw the embarrassment on his face. "Sure, Ms. Destiny. I would love that."

Destiny turned to create space between them.

"Have fuuuuun!" Bliss yelled as they walked away.

"I'm proud of you, baby," Xavier said next to Destiny's ear. He still had his warm body behind her with his arms draped over her shoulders.

"Humph. She better than me," Constance added. She had a drink in her hand as she made her way to the exit.

What a day!

Epilogue

Six months later

Tinsville City Schools were officially in the green. Xavier's face was plastered across the news and several financial magazines. His CEO, Travis Gunther, asked him regularly if he had plans to relocate.

"I told you I'm settled with the family." Xavier understood his concerns. He'd been solicited constantly for jobs that paid a hell of a lot more money than Tinsville did. But he had the privilege to consider more than just his salary. His wife and children thrived in Tinsville. "I'm done for the day. Headed out to see the wife now."

"Grant, it's barely noon," Travis noted.

"I know. The kids are still in school." He winked at Travis who insisted Xavier was like a whipped puppy. Xavier wore the accusation as a badge of honor... because he was.

Their home was less than fifteen minutes from his office.

When he opened the door, his mind filled with all the nasty things he wanted to do to Destiny Grant. Every morning, he was relieved that the past months hadn't been a dream. He woke up with the love of his life in his bed.

"Baby, where you at?" Xavier prayed she hadn't gone to *Upundies*. He was ready for her to quit, but never pressed the issue. He wanted her home for selfish reasons. In his heart, he would support whatever Destiny needed to feel fulfilled. Her job was one of those things.

"I'm in the bedroom," she called down to him.

Xavier's heart thumped and his hands perspired. Zay J, Summer, and Junior had been a handful the past week, and there was little time for Xavier to enjoy his wife. Today, he was aware they had the house to themselves. He took the steps two at a time and berated himself for being so thirsty. When he stepped into the room, he sensed that Destiny was worried about something.

"Everything OK with Jace?" he asked, now concerned himself.

Destiny paced the floor. He'd never seen her this way. He was the one who paced in their relationship. Xavier had seen all of Destiny's emotions—from horny, to grateful, to disappointed, and angry, but he didn't recognize her current mood. *G, protect my wife. Show me how to be here for her. Give me the strength to listen and not fix if that's what she needs. Good looking out!*

"He's fine. He and Bliss are good."

Thank you, G!

Xavier approached her cautiously. "So, what is it, baby? You look worried," Xavier said. He was gentle in his delivery. In the past months, Xavier also saw how sensitive his wife got during her time of the month. *That's got to be what this is about.* If she was on her period, he'd be gentle. That was never enough to keep him from wanting his wife's body.

"You know how you missed out on Jace when he was a baby?"

Xavier exhaled. They'd had this fight too many times. If Xavier asked a question about the past or if Jace talked about a childhood memory, Destiny often got hypervigilant about whether he still blamed her or not. It irritated him because he was a firm believer that two things could be true at once. He could be sad he missed out, and no longer blame her. But convincing her of it was exhausting.

"Baby, I just want to spend time with you while we have the house to ourselves. I don't want to fight."

"Would you want to do sleepless nights and baby clothes?"

"I did it with Zay J. I love that kid, but the experience is a little overrated."

"How do you think the kids would take it?"

Xavier pulled her into him. "Take what, baby?"

"A baby?"

Xavier looked down at her. For the first time, he saw the stick enclosed in a plastic bag in her hands.

"Are you pregnant, Destiny?"

Tears streamed her face. "I got sloppy with my birth control. I hadn't been back to the doctor so—"

Xavier lifted her from her feet and kissed her neck.

"We're too old for this, Zay."

He placed her back on her feet and pulled her face into his hands. "Maybe we are, but we got a gang of helpers."

"Are you upset?"

"Baby." Xavier sat on the bed and pulled Destiny onto his lap. "Are you serious?"

"I know you hate when I nag you about it, but what if this baby reminds you of what you missed with Jace?"

Xavier took a measured breath. "Maybe it will. But I love you. I've forgiven you, and there's nothing I want more than to have this baby with you. If that's what you want. You wanna have my baby... again?"

Destiny nodded as he wiped her tears with the pad of his thumb.

"I love you, Zay."

"I know you do." He kissed her then stood. "You and these kids spend all my damn money."

"Really?" she asked as she grabbed a pillow.

"Stop playing, Destiny," Xavier warned. "Don't hit me with that."

Destiny moved like she would lay it back on the bed but hit him with it instead.

Xavier loosened his tie. "So, you wanna play hide and go get it?"

"You gotta catch me first," she teased.

When Xavier came home, he thought for sure his life couldn't get any better. But now, the woman of his dreams was pregnant with his kid. He was certain it was a boy. He only made boys. If he had it his way, they would fill their home with babies.

As he grabbed Destiny by the hips and pulled her to him, he prayed for them. He prayed for their unborn child and Destiny's pregnancy. Xavier prayed that G would be with their other children in this transition to make room for another Grant. *Thank you, God, for my life and my wife!*

The End

Afterword

Thank you for finishing *Daddy's Maybe*.

If you enjoyed this story, **leave me a five-star rating and review on Amazon, and a positive review on Goodreads,** and **TikTok.** And recommend it to your friends.

Also, I share freebies, sneak peeks, and discounts for sensual products on my mailing list! Sign up here.

http://eepurl.com/h15QoD

Thank you in advance,
Denise Essex

Afterword

Also by Denise Essex

More *Sweet Heat* Reads by Denise 💋

Prison Bae

https://bit.ly/PrisonBaeTrey

The Firemen's Ball: A Masquerade Affair

My Book

The Pleasure Package

https://bit.ly/pleasurepackage

A Naughty Rendezvous

https://bit.ly/ANaughtyRendezvous

Love in the same strip club

https://bit.ly/SameStripClub

Heat Haven Heaux-Tell: Three Novellas

https://bit.ly/HeatHaven

The College Route

https://bit.ly/TheCollegeRoute

I Found Her

https://amzn.to/3VmWLm7

The Visiting Professor

https://bit.ly/TheVisitingProfessor

Gone For a Soldier

https://bit.ly/GoneForASoldier

Let's Connect!

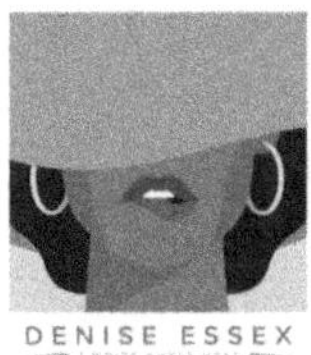

Where to find me in these intanet streets 💋

My readers voted on Daddy's Maybe as the book they wanted me to write next. Join us and give your input!

Readers   Group: https://www.facebook.com/groups/deniseessexheatseekers

Amazon Author Page: https://www.amazon.com/author/denise_essex

Facebook   page: https://www.facebook.com/DeniseEssexAuthor

INSTAGRAM: https://www.instagram.com/deniseessex222/

IG Handle: @DeniseEssex222

TikTok: @DeniseEssex222

Twitter: @DeniseEssex222

BLP

What a time to be a Black girl who loves books!
January 26th-28th, 2024
Memphis, TN
Featuring: The Authors of BLP
Hosted by: B. Love
**To register, click here - https://www.prolificpenpusher.
net/blp-the-gathering**

Visit bit.ly/readBLP to join our mailing list for sneak peeks and
release day links!

B. Love Publications - where Authors celebrate black men, black
women, and black love.
To submit a manuscript for consideration, email your first three
chapters to blovepublications@gmail.com with SUBMISSION as
the subject.

The BLP Podcast – bit.ly/BLPUncovered